crossing the lines

praise for amanda huggins

"Amanda writes with empathy, an eye for vivid detail, a sense of adventure, and great charm."
- Alison Moore, Booker-shortlisted author of *The Lighthouse*

"Amanda Huggins is a writer who understands what makes the world beautiful."
- Tracy Fells, author of *Hairy on the Inside*

Praise for *All Our Squandered Beauty*, winner of the 2021 Saboteur Award for Best Novella:

". . . an affecting portrait of grief in youth. Huggins writes with an attentive, painterly touch for the emotional details of her characters' lives."
- Rónán Hession, author of *Leonard and Hungry Paul* and *Panenka*

"Beauty is never squandered in Huggins's work. This is a writer who grasps it, weaves it through in the details of lives. A powerful story of tides, loss, coming of age, the stories we are told and those we make for ourselves. *All Our Squandered Beauty* is not to be missed. Breathtaking."
- Angela Readman, author of *Something Like Breathing*

crossing
the lines

amanda huggins

Victorina Press
www.victorinapress.com

Typesetting and layout: Jorge Vasquez
Cover design: Triona Walsh

British Library Cataloguing in Publication Data
A catalogue record for this book is available from the
British Library.

ISBN: 978-1-9169057-1-9

Typeset in 12pt Garamond
Printed and bound in Great Britain by 4edge Ltd.

For everyone who has ever had to cut and run – and for all those who are still running or have yet to set off

contents

across five state lines

Sherman Rook walked into the Jupiter diner one quiet Thursday afternoon, ordered coffee and a slice of cherry pie. He stood with both hands on the chipped Formica counter, tilted his head to one side and told Ella Archer that she put him in mind of somebody.

'I'm sure it's a Hollywood film star, or maybe a country singer,' he said.

Mollie watched her mama blush as she reached up to adjust her hair, heard her say she hoped it was someone real pretty.

When Ella went across to his table with the coffee jug, Sherman said he'd remembered who it was. Mollie put down her tray and paused to listen, yet it turned out to be the girl he'd taken to his high school prom – no one famous after all.

'She was the prettiest girl in the whole darn school,' he said, and Mollie curled up inside with embarrassment. But her mama took the compliment and swallowed it whole, threw back her head and laughed, as though offering her pale throat to a prowling lion.

He came by again at the close of day, freshly shaved, wearing a clean plaid shirt still criss-crossed with creases from the packet. It was a little tight around the chest and he'd turned back the cuffs to reveal a watch studded with gimcrack crystals which sparkled under the lights. He tapped his left foot as he talked, drawing attention to snakeskin cowboy boots with gold toe rands. Mollie noticed his voice had a vague southern drawl to it and a nasal whine which made him sound a little mean.

He took her mama out to the new clam restaurant five miles down the shore, and Mollie heard their laughter when he dropped her off at midnight, a schmalzy country tune drifting out from the open window of his pickup.

Sherman Rook was only in town for three nights, but he took her mama for dinner on the Friday and Saturday as well, and on Sunday morning Mollie heard his voice through the thin wall between their bedrooms. She knew there and then that Mama must be serious about him, as she normally made sure her men friends left the house well before she thought Mollie would be awake, shushing them at the kitchen door, whispering her goodbyes.

Mollie pulled on a swimming costume and shorts, climbed out of her window onto the porch and walked down to the boardwalk. She perched up on the railings at her favourite spot, the place where she'd often hung out with her brother Angel when they were kids. From there she could still watch the house as well as the ocean, and she listened to the rhythmic crash and pull of the waves until long after Sherman's green Ford disappeared down Sunset Street.

When she arrived back home she could see straight away that Mama was radiant, happier than she'd looked since the day Daddy left. Yet Mollie couldn't help but shiver, even though she wasn't entirely sure why.

She fixed a jug of coffee and warmed some pancakes, sat down at the table, her mama all the while talking about Sherman Rook. She said he lived way out west, but he'd be back in three weeks' time.

Mollie would have put money on him never

returning, would have staked her shell collection and her favourite Springsteen T-shirt, the novelty ring out of a Thanksgiving cracker that Perry Slade had given to her in sixth grade.

But he did return, on a sultry Friday afternoon, and as soon as he arrived he asked them to move out to Oakridge Farm, Boulton County. Mollie knew she'd never forget the date. She'd always been superstitious – taking three steps back when a black cat walked across her path, throwing spilt salt into the devil's face – and the day Sherman Rook asked them to move was Friday 13th July 1979, only a few weeks before her fifteenth birthday.

Neither of them listened when Mollie said she wanted to stay behind and move in with her daddy or Angel. That was when Sherman put his arm around her shoulders, looked her up and down as if seeing her for the first time. Something in his eyes glittered hard and bright as he appraised her cloud of unruly blonde hair, the jut of her determined chin and her long, tanned legs.

Before the week was out they gathered everything they needed into two old suitcases and half a dozen packing crates. Mollie went down to Atlantic City to visit her daddy one last time, then Mama told Benny Dee she was quitting her job at the diner and arranged for their house to be let.

Mollie sat between them in the pickup, the backs of her legs sticking to the quilted bench seat, and every so often she felt Sherman's hand brush her knee, flinched as the rough callous on his right palm scraped against her skin. Once, at a gas station, when he reached across to the glovebox, his other hand slipped between her legs and pinched the tender skin on her inner thigh.

Yet Mama never noticed a thing.

They drove for two solid days across five state lines to reach Oakridge, the dull thrum· of the truck lulling Mollie to sleep in the heat of the afternoons no matter how hard she tried to stay awake. They stopped overnight at a cheap motel with stained carpets and broken blinds, a dusty hosepipe coiled like a rattlesnake by the empty pool.

Sherman asked for connecting rooms and left the adjoining door wide open. Mollie undressed in her bathroom, slid the bolt across just in case, then climbed silently into bed, feeling every spring of the worn mattress, listening out for his snores before she dared to fall asleep herself. She knew for certain that when they reached Oakridge Farm it would be exactly like this; she would lie awake each and every night, and on one of those nights her world would change and no one would save her.

beachcombing

They skirted brash-bright cities, drove through one-trick towns, crossed county line after county line, the urban landscapes changing as quickly as the nature of the countryside in between them. The ice cream parlours and ocean-themed cafés were replaced by functional diners and burger joints; the chandlers and surf shops were swapped for hardware stores, truck stops, outdoor outfitters.

Mollie already knew she would miss her daddy's boatyard, the warm sand between her toes, the wide stretch of sky and the endless tug of the waves. The sand had been replaced by a fine dust which coated the windscreen in a rusty film that Sherman constantly washed away with the wipers. At first she still heard the cries of the gulls in her head, but soon they were silenced, exchanged for the rough caw and cackle of lone crows searching for scraps on fast food forecourts.

When she was younger, Mollie had gone down to her daddy's boatyard most days after school. They would walk the length of the empty beach together in the late afternoon, gathering shells and pebbles, driftwood for the stove, coils of frayed rope. Mollie's favourite treasures were those things the sea had taken and fashioned anew: rumbled sea glass turned into sapphires, emeralds and amber, rounded nubs of broken china. She imagined the nuggets of glass were precious stones washed up from the bowels of shipwrecks — jewels from the tiaras and necklaces of wealthy ladies. She could hear the rustle of their skirts as they stepped out across dance floors in velvet slippers, their diamonds catching the light beneath chandeliers; imagined them waking in the night to the crash and roil of the sea, the screams and shouts outside the cabin, the groan of the ship as it sank beneath the waves. She saw the whites of their terrified eyes as they ran along corridors in their embroidered nightgowns, hair streaming behind them, abandoned possessions swept along in the rising water.

After their walks, Mollie would spread her homework out on the sagging blue couch in the boatyard office, and in winter her daddy would light the potbelly stove that stood in the corner. They made cocoa topped with toasted mallows, and the girl at the cookie bakery always saved a bag of chocolate chip bites for them. Other than customers, no one ever came there to disturb them, not even Mama. Mollie knew her mother liked it when they were both out of her way, preferred it when there was just Angel at home. Her brother had always been Mama's favourite, but she'd never really minded as long as she had Daddy.

Then, one summer, Janet Pearlman appeared on the beach.

She arrived from nowhere with a battered surfboard and a gap-toothed grin, wearing a towelling beach robe patterned with palm trees and flamingos. On the afternoons she was around, Mollie noticed her daddy was always smiling, that he had one eye on his work and the other on Janet. He said he knew her from way back when, that she lived down in Longfield near Atlantic City and was working at Ged's barbershop a few mornings a week.

Janet surfed for hours when the waves were

right, and Mollie lay on her stomach and watched her from the boatyard decking, copying her moves as she paddled out against the tide. When the ocean was flat she swam the length of the bay and Mollie admired the way her arms sliced through the water, the quiet power of her breaststroke. She was as one with the sea – a mermaid – and when Mollie said as much to her daddy, she noticed how he smiled to himself, a little coy, as though accepting a compliment on Janet's behalf.

Up close, Mollie could see Janet was more than simply pretty, yet she showed no sign of being aware of her beauty. She had high cheekbones, her long hair was thick and glossy, her eyes a soft grey. She wore a handful of gold chains around her left wrist that glittered in the sun.

Janet pressed the tips of her fingers to Daddy's hand when she talked to him, let her hair fall forward to brush his cheek, passed him tools as he worked, sang softly to him when she thought Mollie was out of earshot. Yet Mollie was both watching and listening, already aware of something tightening inside her chest. She could feel the wind of change blowing in from the ocean.

tunnel vision

Ella Archer pulled aside the parlour curtains and looked out across the endless roll of the plains beyond Oakridge. The morning was hot for late summer and the fields appeared to shimmer on the horizon.

The day Sherman Rook first came into the Jupiter diner had been one of the hottest that year. The road leading to the beach quivered with mirages, and the strip of melting blacktop hovered above the surrounding dunes. Ella pressed her wrists to the bags of ice before she split them open, rolled chilled bottles of water across her forehead and the back of her neck. When Sherman walked in she was almost too tired to care about another out-of-town cowboy, too hot to flirt or make small talk, but nevertheless her hands automatically smoothed her apron and adjusted her hair as she switched on the prettiest of her well-practised smiles.

Everyone on the north shore knew Ella Archer had a thing for older men – or that was certainly the way it looked. Some folks said she was searching for a sugar daddy, and those who were kinder suggested she was simply looking for someone to take care of her now her husband was living near Atlantic City with his childhood sweetheart.

There were others who said she was little better than a hooker, yet Ella made sure she never took money from the men she dated – at least not the kind of money which could be construed as direct payment. The only time that had happened was when she was fourteen years old and didn't know any better. And when she met

Phil Archer she took care not to let him find out about all those boys she'd slept with before.

Yet Ella knew just how easy it was to extract money from men, and since she'd been on her own again she'd learnt ways to take it that satisfied her conscience, ways of kidding herself it was something else. She acted affronted if they tried to leave money discreetly on the bedside table, but when they offered her cash to buy herself something pretty, well, that was different. She didn't see it as a payment for services rendered, but viewed it as a gift from a friend. And she'd like someone to show her the girl who'd refuse a gift.

The men Ella brought home were sometimes married, but more usually they were divorcees. She attracted a type – often a little out of shape, flash and brash, men who wore pinkie rings glinting with chunky stones, wiped their brows with paisley handkerchiefs. They took her dancing to Amy's Roadhouse, watched her like a hawk in case she flirted with the younger men from the construction site at Owen Falls. They drank bottled beer and bourbon chasers, listened to country and western music, told her stories about the ex-wives who'd taken them for every cent, about their Irish daddies who'd fallen foul of the bottle. And when they tired of Ella trying to pin them down, or they found themselves a prettier woman to hook on their arm, she never wasted any time before taking up with someone else. Yet every replacement was the same as the last.

When Sherman Rook came into the diner he appeared to be exactly like all the others – albeit a little more polished, smoother around the edges, slightly better-looking. Yet she already sensed something else beneath his veneer of sweet talk. There was a harder edge he was trying not to show, a coldness behind his smile. She could almost feel the temperature fall, half-expected to see his breath clouding the air. But Ella didn't heed the signs; she had tunnel vision as she listened to his spiel, and at the other end of that tunnel she spied a fine house like something out of *Gone With the Wind* and a roll of dollars as thick as her wrist.

Over dinner he told her more about his farmstead, the wide sunsets and the rolling plains, the porticoed house that was once his late parents' home – his mother a Southern belle, his pa some big-shot rancher who'd retired to Boulton County from further out west. He told her he was looking for a little lady to make the house a home again. That should have been Ella's warning, but something inside her ached with the want of this fancy farm in Oakridge. She had an urge to abandon sense and consequences, to move far away from the endless grating sound of the waves as they pulled back through the shingle. She could hear a low trill inside her head as he talked, like a quiet alarm bell, and a cold shiver ran through every ridge of her spine. Yet Ella still wanted all of this, craved everything he had to offer. She liked the way he poured her wine, chose her food, placed his hand over hers as he talked. She told herself she needed his old-fashioned values, that his strong hands would make her safe.

On their third date he told her he made love like a man should, the way he knew women wanted it, and he'd make no apology for that. And when he held her down by her wrists, pushed straight inside her, she told herself it was exciting, passionate, that he couldn't wait, couldn't help himself.

The following day, when Sherman had driven back to his hotel to check out, she lay awake and pondered the price of living in a fine homestead five states west. She knew the cost could be high, but somehow his fancy wine had been enough to dilute her doubts.

It was the morning they left Sunset Street, as she lifted her suitcase into the back of his pickup, that Ella Archer first noticed the way Sherman Rook looked at her daughter. She hesitated a second before reaching for the door handle of the cab, but she'd quit her job for this, bragged to her friends about her exciting new life, and if she didn't want to lose face then she had no choice but to go. She told herself she'd have to make the best of it, yet somehow she hadn't, and the words she wanted to say were always stuck to her tongue, choked off by the dust of Oakridge Farm.

counting to fifty

Mollie sat on the porch step and kicked up the dust with the toe of her boot. The Oakridge dust was ox red, as though stained with the blood of those who had worked the land before. It was a dust so fine you could trace patterns in it with a blade of grass, and when the rains came it thickened into a paste that dyed your skin like henna.

Sherman Rook had told Mama he was in the automobile business, that he had money and a fine house with a parcel of land. Yet it turned out he owned a used car lot, and his rundown ranch was little finer than their own two-bit clapboard house.

They'd lived at Oakridge for six weeks and two days now, Mollie had seen the stray dog twenty-nine days in a row, and last night was the seventh time Sherman had tried to come into her room.

She opened her diary and recorded the new totals in three ruled columns on the back page, writing the numbers with the souvenir pen her daddy had bought in Atlantic City the last time she'd seen him. He'd bought salt water taffy that day too, and she'd saved the box. It was the old-fashioned kind with bathing belles on the lid, and it was where she kept her diary and her collection of mud snail shells. Every evening she wrote about the stray dog and how close to the house he'd come that day. She described the changing colours of the sky, confessed how much she missed Angel and her daddy. More than ever before she wished she could still talk to Chrissy, the only true friend she'd ever had.

She didn't write about Sherman, about how scared she was that the loose bolt on her door wouldn't hold out, how she'd taken a screwdriver from his toolbox to try to tighten it, and how she'd hidden that screwdriver safely beneath her pillow.

The porch steps were her favourite place to sit. There was a wooden tub filled with the same flowers that Mama used to grow outside the house back home, those white blooms with a sweet, powdery scent that flowered all summer. And the smell of them at Oakridge always caught Mollie unawares, taking her straight back to Sunset Street and the boardwalk.

They were over a thousand miles from the shore now. Sherman Rook had certainly wasted no time before asking her mother to move out to Oakridge, and Mama had given her answer in front of Mollie and all the customers in the Jupiter diner.

"Can't bear to be without you one minute longer, Ella Archer!" he'd said, and Mama had smiled her pretty smile and said yes right away. That was when Mollie had stepped out of the tiny kitchen and said she'd rather stay with Angel and his girlfriend, or down at her daddy's house. Sherman put his arm around her shoulders, squeezed a little too tightly for a little too long and declared she would do no such thing.

And now, on the nights when he stayed late in town, she spread out his road map on the floor, traced her finger along the route east until she knew the name of every town on every highway that led back to the shore, imagined crossing the lines from one county to the next, counting them off, on and on, until she reached New Jersey.

When she heard the slam of the pickup door, the creak and swing of the porch screen, Sherman staggering along the hallway, she pushed the map underneath her bed and waited. If his footsteps paused outside her room, Mollie held her breath and reached for the screwdriver. She waited for him to weigh up his options, told herself that if she could count to fifty before he reached for the handle then he would keep right on walking to Mama's room. Often it worked, yet sometimes she didn't count past ten before he rattled the door, and then she covered her ears and recited the names of the counties in her head.

pretty

Ella Jones lost her virginity to Mr Clark at the age of fourteen.

She'd never even had a boyfriend, knew little about kissing and nothing about making out, but she was giddy to know it all. She wanted to grow up fast, to wear her hair piled up on top of her head like Olivia Clark, to kiss the boys in the dunes, soft sand falling away beneath them, warm wind whispering through the marram grass at dusk.

She took the bus over to Olivia's one Saturday afternoon and caught her kissing Andrew Devine, pressed up against the garage wall, her skirt bunched around her waist. She knew Ella was watching them and she ground her hips against him until he let out a low moan. Then she turned her head and smiled at Ella, told Andrew she'd meet him for the drive-in movie on Sunday night.

When Ella said she wished she had Olivia's looks, her style, her sassy wit, Olivia laughed that perfect laugh, the one which started off breathy, all Marilyn Monroe, and finished clear and high as temple bells. She tucked Ella's hair behind her ear and told her she was pretty. She swore she'd die for her perfect skin, would kill for her short, neat hair and those perfect bangs. So classy, she said, so grown-up.

Olivia invited Ella to stay over that night, and when her parents went to bed she fetched her mother's hairdressing scissors from the bathroom cabinet. She placed a chair in the middle of the bedroom floor and asked Ella to give her bangs exactly like her own. Ella combed Olivia's hair over her face, told her to shut her eyes before she started to chop. She cut the bangs in three sharp snips, gloried at the sight of her friend's thick blonde hair falling onto the rug. She said she would trim the length too, then she clipped the sides, the back, shorter and shorter, wielding the scissors as fast as she could while Olivia's eyes were still closed.

When she opened them again she saw the jagged pile of hair on the floor, blonde hanks cascading over her lap. And when Olivia screamed, Ella explained that all she'd been doing was cutting her hair until it was as short as her own, so now she didn't have to kill for it after all.

Mrs Clark's lips formed a thin slit, the colour of putty, and her words, as they rushed out under pressure, were the hiss and growl of a coffee machine. She called Ella's parents from the hallway phone, stood in her nightdress in the drive, arms crossed, as Mr Clark reversed the car.

As they set off through the dark countryside he put his hand on Ella's knee, told her not to worry. And she knew it was going to be alright, because Mr Clark said she was pretty too. He said she was the prettiest of all the girls.

birthday present

Sherman Rook soon tired of Ella Archer. He was smitten with her at the start, so sure he had found his perfect match. She was the kind of woman who fitted right in with that old saying about being a whore in the bedroom, a maid in the parlour and a cook in the kitchen; still young enough to keep him interested, though not so young that she'd turn out flighty.

Yet Ella lost her shine when he took her away from the New Jersey shore. Instead of sweeping the pale sand from the Jupiter doorway, she was constantly brushing the red dust of Oakridge Farm from the hallway and the kitchen. The dust even blew under the door into the green gloom of the parlour, where the fringed curtains were permanently drawn against the sun, just as they'd been in Sherman's mother's time. The dust coated Ella's tongue and teeth, settled in her hair and the pores of her skin. Without the diner to run, and with her family and friends five states east, she became eaten up with loneliness.

Sherman was out from early morning until late evening, and sometimes he stayed away all night, so Mollie and Ella were often left to their own devices. They took the local bus into town because Mama didn't drive. Mollie knew how to – her daddy had shown her last summer when they were out in the backwoods – but Sherman wasn't about to let a fourteen-year-old girl behind the wheel of one of his pickup trucks, let alone his station wagon. So they walked down the track to the highway, their shoes coated in dust that left rusty footprints along the aisle of the bus.

On Mollie's fifteenth birthday they asked in the hardware store if there was a good place for lunch and were directed to Lily Brown's. Mama pursed her lips as soon as they walked through the door and Mollie could see they'd been set up. The customers were all men, no one was eating. Sherman Rook was sitting at the bar with his arm around one of the barmaids. Mama turned on her heel before he even looked up, led Mollie across the road to Joe's Subs. Neither of them said a word, yet they'd both heard the laughter that followed them down the street.

When Sherman came home that evening he slammed the door hard enough to shake the lucky horseshoe free from the lintel. He pulled Mama inside their room without a word, then Mollie heard the swish and snap of his belt. She stayed quiet and still by the parlour window, hoped he would forget she was there, yet not five minutes later he crashed through the door and grabbed Mollie by the wrists, pinning them together with the span of one hand. Even though she screamed, her mama didn't come, and she turned her face away from the sourness of Sherman's breath as he swung back his arm.

And after that night, Mollie began to despise her mama's weakness; the way her silence made her complicit, the way she appeared to offer no resistance. At first Mollie tried to talk to her, stroking the bruises on her wrists, saying they should go back home. But when Mama acted as though she hadn't heard, gazed out across the fields just as she'd stared out to sea after Daddy left, Mollie understood that if she were to see the shore again she'd have to find some way of getting there alone. Sometimes she hated herself for having so little courage. She felt powerless, as though she had no choice but to bide her time, just as thousands of women did every day, even though the same bad things kept on happening to them, even though promise after promise was broken. It was her mama who used to say that once a line had been crossed there was no going back. Yet time after time that line was being re-drawn inside her head; it was as though she was waiting for some elusive decider before she could act, as though she would recognise this ultimate line as the deal-breaker the moment it was stepped over, but not before.

saul

One Friday morning, before her mama was even dressed, Mollie heard a knock on the front door. No one ever came up to Oakridge save for the delivery man from the store, and he always went round to the kitchen. She looked through the parlour window and saw a blue pickup she didn't recognise. When she opened the door there was no one there.

Mollie stepped outside, watched a boy of nineteen or twenty rolling a tyre across to Rook's station wagon. He saw her and stopped, lifted a hand as if to wave, then propped the tyre up against the driver's door. He walked back across the yard, shading his eyes from the low sun, stopped short a little way from the porch steps.

'Saul Bradshaw,' he said. 'I work for your father.'

'He's not my father.'

He coloured up and rubbed the back of his neck. 'No, that is, I . . . sorry, miss . . . well, I work for Sherman Rook anyways, and I'm over here to swap his tyres.'

Mollie nodded and sat down on the bench. She watched him work, studied the muscles in his forearms, the strength in his shoulders as he crouched down at the side of the car, the way his T-shirt rode up, pulled free from his belt as he cranked the jack. Every now and then he looked over at her and smiled. When he stood up again she noticed how tall he was, the way he hunched over a little as though he was trying to take up less space in the world.

She was sorry she hadn't been more friendly.

'Would you like me to fetch you a coffee?' she shouted.

He straightened up and walked over to her again, came a little closer this time so she could see the cornflower blue of his eyes. They were kind eyes, she thought, the sort of eyes that belonged to a person you could trust. He would look after a girl, be dependable, take care to make sure you were okay, never hurt you on purpose. When Saul met her gaze, the hairs stood up on the back of her neck.

'No thank you, miss. It sure is nice of you to offer, but I'm almost done here and Mr Rook needs me back at the car lot pretty fast.'

She nodded. 'I should have asked sooner.'

When she watched him drive away an empty place opened up inside her, as though she'd let something important slip through her grasp.

•

hal

The Oakridge house crouched on the brow of a hill. It was in need of a lick of paint, bare-boned and weathered, hidden from view by a stand of trees until you turned the last bend in the track. Mollie hated the dark, brooding weight of it, the trees so dense they held a part of the night's heart within them even when the sun shone.

Yet beyond the house, the land dipped and rolled as far as the eye could see, endless plains stretching out towards the county line. And the sky over the fields was as wide as the sky over the Atlantic Ocean. Mollie watched it change colour from blush to the darkest ink, wondered if Daddy and Angel were watching that same piece of sky five states east. In the mornings she'd see eagles hover over the red earth, and in the half-light of dusk she'd glimpse the shifting shapes of animals crossing the land: cottontails, coyote, lone stray dogs.

At night Mollie would listen to the haunting calls of owls, the eerie howl and yip of the dogs. Yet they didn't scare her. What scared her was the bang of the screen door, the key turning in the lock, the heave and grunt of Sherman Rook as he rattled her bedroom door.

Most nights she was spared. Those nights when Sherman was too drunk and she'd hear him clatter along the hallway, the long case clock clanging as the weights jangled, his muttered curse when he tripped over the row of boots. Those nights when he went straight to her mama and she could hear the rhythmic creak of the bed through the wall. And the best nights: the nights when he was so drunk he didn't come back at all, but stayed at Lily Brown's bar.

On the mornings he was home, Sherman got up before first light, was away to the car lot by seven. And then the day was Mollie's to do as she pleased. She walked the paths that ran along the perimeter of the fields, tried to capture the elusive colours of the earth and sky with her oil pastels and watercolour paints.

It was late afternoon the first time she saw the stray dog. His coat was as red as the earth, with a streak of white at the throat like the blaze of a comet, and his face was as long as a fox's snout. At first she thought he was a young coyote, but his shape was wrong – too short in the body and legs – and his colour too dense. He lifted each paw high as he trotted along the edge of the field. Mollie caught a glimpse of him by the fence, their eyes met briefly and he was gone. She christened him Halley – Hal for short – after the only comet she'd heard named.

The next time Mollie telephoned the town store she added a bag of dog kibble to their grocery order, and her mama didn't question it. She left a small handful close to where she'd first seen Hal, then watched from the window until she saw his face peer out between the ears of wild wheat. His nose twitched as he caught the smell of the biscuits, he slid under the fence into the yard, his ears cocked and his head turning at the slightest sound. Each day she moved the kibble a little closer to the house, and now, on day thirty, Hal had stepped right up to her open window. The chickens caught his scent and shuffled and clucked in their coop. She saw the glint of his clear, sharp eyes, his damp nose, the thick fur of his tail, matted with red earth and burrs.

'Hal,' she whispered. She held out her arm, rested it on the low sill, and he came to her, tame yet shy, and let her stroke his flank, the fur unfeasibly soft.

That night she made sketches of him in her diary and coloured them with the muddied squares of paint in her watercolour box. On the back page she added to her tally: six weeks and three days living at Oakridge, and the thirtieth day of seeing Hal. Sherman had stayed at Lily Brown's last night, so the third column still stood at seven.

Seven times he'd rattled her door, whispered her name in a drunken slur, pleaded for her to let him in. And seven times Mollie had stayed silent, feigned sleep, prayed the bolt would hold as she reached for the screwdriver under her pillow, held it so tightly in her fist she feared her bones would crack.

She put the diary back inside her taffy box and climbed into bed. Then she lay down and waited.

our secret for all time

Angel sat on the boardwalk railings, watched the sun appear out of the waves. He rolled a cigarette with one hand, then slipped the tobacco pouch back into his pocket. The heavy clunk of his lighter, the flare of the flame, the first deep drag, they were all part of his morning ritual; his thinking time.

He could see his mama's house from there, the familiar, comforting shape of his childhood home, and for a moment he thought he saw a shadow move across the kitchen window. Perhaps the agent had already rented it out and someone new was living there.

He took out Mollie's latest letter from Boulton County. He wished he could read between the lines, could work out how she was really doing out there. She told him about the wide skies, the calls of birds she couldn't name, the red dust that settled into your skin like face powder, how she missed the sound of the sea. And then she told him how Sherman had kindly said Mama could teach her at home, which Angel thought didn't quite ring true. God bless his mama, but she sure wasn't bright enough to teach high school kids.

Mollie always listed the minute details of her day: what she had eaten for dinner, the names she'd given the chickens, the colour of the curtains Mama was sewing for the kitchen windows. But these paragraphs were stilted and dry; they didn't sound like Mollie's voice. When she signed off, she explained each time how she'd be sending their mail down to the post office with Sherman Rook, and Angel guessed she thought he might be reading her letters, that she wasn't able to tell him the whole story. Intuition told him something was amiss, that there was a truth he needed to discover, hidden by this outer shell. He thought of Mollie's letters as fragile birds' eggs, containing secrets he couldn't quite see even when he held them up to the light.

He shivered when he remembered the egg he once stole from a nest in the dunes.

He'd been around nine or ten at the time, entrusted to look after his little sister for the very first time. Mama had told them not to go far, but he wanted to show Mollie the secret place he'd found at the far end of the beach. A tiny oval dip, framed by marram grass, sheltered and invisible from the path. He took her hand and led her over the dunes, laughing as her short legs sank into the fine sand.

There were four eggs in the nest they stumbled across: pale blue and freckled. The mother had flown off in a panicked whir of wings when she heard Angel and Mollie approach. He didn't even know what kind of bird it was.

Mollie held his arm as they peered into the nest.

'I hope the mama bird will come back,' she said, 'before the eggs get cold.'

They shaded their eyes and scanned the sky for signs of her, but the expanse of blue was empty. Angel bent down and picked up one of the eggs, held it in his open palm for Mollie to see.

'Put it back!' she said anxiously. 'The mama won't like it if we touch it.'

'That's just silly folklore, Mollie. How come you

30

know so much about birds anyhow?'

'Daddy told me,' she said. 'Daddy said I was never to touch a nest.'

'Well I can't put this one back then,' said Angel, decisively. 'If I put it back now then the others will be abandoned too.'

He wrapped it in his handkerchief and slipped it into his pocket. Mollie still looked worried.

'Don't fret, Mollie. It won't be a bird yet – just some gloop. It's not as though I've killed anything.'

Back home he took the egg out and turned it around in his hand. He would blow it later, just like that time Billy blew a gull's egg. In fact he might ask his friend to come round, to make sure he did it right. He fetched a pin from Mama's sewing box and carried the egg into his parents' room, holding it up against the bright reading light next to his daddy's side of the bed. Billy's egg had a dark spot in the centre that he said was the start of the baby bird. But Angel's was different. It was almost completely dark inside, as though it was solid. He imagined he could make out the outline of a baby bird, like a tiny dinosaur curled up tight. For a moment he regretted taking it from the nest. There could be a bird inside there after all. A bird which would never open its wings, would never see the bright, endless width of the sky, a bird which would never soar and swoop, or glide on the currents, would never take in the boardwalk, the ocean, the sky, in a single dive.

He called Billy's house, but his mother said he was out with his cousin, so he decided to do it alone. He went back into his bedroom and carefully tapped the pin into the top of the egg, pushed it right through and twisted it around to break up the yolk, just as he'd seen Billy do. But the pin was catching on something solid. He turned it upside down to make the second hole in the bottom. As he tapped the pin again, Mollie walked into his room, her eyes widening when she saw what he was doing.

'Sit down and watch. I'm going to blow the yolk out of the bottom,' he said.

Yet as he carefully twisted the pin in the bottom hole, he felt something solid again, and as he pulled it back out, the shell cracked into a dozen pieces and fell away, revealing a tiny pink beak, an eye like a jet bead, a mess of purple flesh and wet feather stumps.

Mollie stared at it for a moment in morbid fascination, then stood up and backed towards the door.

'You killed it!' she said, her eyes widening in disbelief. 'You killed the baby bird – Mama and Daddy are going to be so mad with you.'

'Don't say anything! Mollie, please don't? I'll make it okay.'

The next morning, Angel took Mollie back to the dunes. They crept up quietly so as not to frighten the mother bird, and as they approached the nest Mollie could hear the tiny cries of a hatchling. Angel reached silently for his sister's hand and pulled her back.

'They'll be okay,' he whispered.

When they got home, Angel wrapped the dead bird in his old flannel and they buried it at the bottom of the yard in a cracker box. As they walked back to the house, Mollie made the sign of the cross.

'Our secret for all time?' asked Angel.

Mollie nodded, and neither of them spoke of

the baby bird again. They both sensed that if their secret were ever mentioned, something between them would break, just like the egg. They were bound together by a small sadness.

attuned to the wind

Mollie tried not to close her eyes until she was certain Sherman Rook was home and asleep. She preferred to lie awake until he arrived back from Lily Brown's, to steel herself as she heard his footsteps along the corridor, waiting for the pause outside her bedroom. It was somehow so much worse to be woken by him already cursing as he rattled her door.

As she waited she thought about the stray dog; how he'd finally let her stroke him, how she yearned to walk free as he did, roaming the plains on silent paws, attuned to the wind in the wheat. Mollie wanted to leave Oakridge Farm and keep right on going, to escape the red dust, the weight of the house, Sherman Rook's crooked smile, the way he looked at her, the sweat and heft of him. She would walk all the way to the shore if she had to.

In the stillness she thought she heard Hal's soft bark from beyond the trees, and as her eyes closed Mollie's last waking thought was to wonder if he was as lonely and scared as she was herself.

Just before dawn she was woken by the rattle of a key in the lock. Mollie listened as Sherman crashed into the house. The screen door bounced twice against the jamb; she heard a scrabbling in the hallway followed by the bang of the frame again. She lay still, held her breath, clenched her fists until the nails bit into her flesh. Finally, she heard quiet footsteps on the porch, boots treading carefully.

He had gone back outside.

There was a squawking in the henhouse, then the crack of a single bullet. She parted the curtains, saw Sherman running up the porch steps, silver-grey in the half-light, holding his gun over the crook of his arm.

Their eyes met through the window. She dropped the curtain and grabbed her boots, but he was too fast. He kicked her bedroom door so hard that the frame cracked and the bolt burst open. In one hand he held his leather belt, and with the other he threw a handful of kibble that stung her face like hailstones.

After he'd gone, she lay down on the bed. She knew her mother must be awake, yet even now she didn't come in to check if Mollie was okay. She waited until she could hear Sherman snoring through the thin wall. Then she dressed quickly, took her taffy box and the road map, a twenty-dollar bill her daddy had given her for emergencies, her rust sweater that matched the colour of Hal's coat.

She walked softly across the yard, her boots already streaked red with the dew-damp earth. The dog's body lay at the side of the barn. She walked over, bent down to him, traced a finger along his fur until she felt the congealed blood on his side, then pulled her hand away. It wasn't him. The fur was coarse and thick, and Mollie could see it was the body of a half-grown coyote. She could smell the metallic tang of blood on her fingers, could feel the welts left by Sherman's belt, yet her heart still soared. It no longer mattered that she was stained with the red of Oakridge, because the dog wasn't Hal.

As she passed the pickup she saw Sherman had left the keys in the ignition. She glanced back at the house one last time; it crouched behind her in reassuring darkness. The truck was pointing down the hill, so she had a chance. Mollie swung up into the cab and let the handbrake off slowly. It rolled forward a few feet, almost stopped, then gradually picked up momentum. She steered carefully down the track, not daring to start the engine until she reached the highway. At the junction she saw the dark red silhouette of a dog sitting in the centre of the road, his eyes a luminous milky green in her headlights. Mollie reached across and opened the passenger door. He stood, sniffed the air, held a single paw aloft for a moment, then trotted over to the truck and jumped straight in.

let him know he's yours

The dawn sky is umber, the faintest stars are still visible above the ghost of a moon. There's nothing on the road and the needle tells Mollie she has the best part of a tank of gas. Yet she knows she'll have to leave the pickup behind as soon as she can, before Sherman Rook discovers it's missing and comes after her. She turns on the radio; a mellow voice drifts over her like a comfort blanket, as hypnotic as the wheels turning and the drone of the engine. The DJ sounds kind. She wants to call up the station, talk to him and ask him what she should do. Yet even though he sounds kind he might tell her to go back, not believe her when she explains what happened.

She's pretty sure Sherman won't catch up with her now. He's unlikely to be awake until the afternoon after an all-night session at the bar. She has maybe two or three hours before the roads will be busy, and then she risks being pulled over by a state trooper. But Mollie knows her emergency twenty dollars is not enough to get to the shore by bus, and there's nothing worth selling in the back of the pickup: half a crate of beer, a coil of rope, an empty canvas knapsack, a few tools in a battered tin box.

She sees a roadhouse up ahead, two men stacking boxes outside the back door in the half-light. Mollie swings into the parking lot at the last moment, tyres churning the grit. She walks over with the half crate of beer, rests it down on the dusty tarmac, asks if they want to buy it.

The tall one looks her up and down for a

moment, wipes a film of sweat from his forehead with the back of his hand.

'Are you in some kind of trouble?'

'No. I just . . .'

He shakes his head and looks back at the pickup. She's parked sideways, so he can't read the plates, but she catches something in his expression, can see that he knows. She picks up the crate again, starts to walk away, staggering backwards a few paces before turning towards the truck.

'Say, ain't that Rook's pickup?'

She throws the beer onto the seat next to Hal and drives off in a cloud of dust, her heart pounding.

A Springsteen song plays on the radio, and she yearns for the boardwalk, for the twilight hour when the lights blink on along the shoreline, for all those stories of corner boys and barefoot girls. The only thing that matters is making it back to the coast; she can feel the ache of it in her throat.

The sun has crept up above the rim of the plains now, yet the air is still cool. Mollie notices the leaves are starting to turn yellow, realises summer is all but over. The road is wide and empty, and she drives on, as fast as she feels safe, putting as many miles as she dare between her and Sherman Rook.

Eventually she stops at a gas station, parks around the side and goes into the restroom. When she comes out she sees the owner watching her from the shop window. He's an old guy with an honest face. She swings the crate of beer out of the truck again and walks over to the door.

'Do you want to buy any beer?' she asks.

He looks at Mollie's face, smeared with dust, takes in the dog standing on the forecourt, his eyes never leaving the girl.

'What exactly are you running from, miss?'

'Nothing,' she says, a little too quickly. 'I'm not running from anything.'

'Then what are you running to?'

She pauses. 'Well . . . the ocean I guess. My daddy maybe. My brother, Angel.'

He stares at her for a minute, the clock ticking, Hal still watching through the glass door.

'Could I trade the beer for a drink and a snack?' she asks. 'Some dog food maybe?'

He reaches underneath the counter and pulls out a box of kibble, then walks slowly along the back of the shop, taking his time. He picks up a bag of pretzels, a sandwich from the cooler, a bottle of water, pushes them into a paper sack.

'Here, these are on the house.' He jerks his head towards the pickup. 'I think I can guess what you're running from. So keep the beer for when you really need it. And that dog out there, that dog yours?'

She nods.

'Then you need to get him a collar. Let him know he's yours, keep him out of trouble.'

'Well you might know I haven't the money for a collar.'

He sighs, looks out through the door again, then reaches back under the counter and brings out a red collar.

'Here,' he says. 'I don't need this no more.'

She picks it up, reads the metal tag. 'This says

Bert. My dog's name is Hal.'

'That so?' He reaches across for the collar, slips his nail between the split ring and lets the tag fall onto the counter.

'There you go. Now he can be Hal, Bert, Fred, whatever goddam name you want him to be.'

She grins and drops it into the bag. 'Thanks.'

He nods. As she opens the door, he calls her back. 'You need to ditch the pickup as soon as you can – you don't need me to tell you that.'

When she slips the collar around Hal's neck she expects him to wriggle away, but he stands still as she fiddles with the buckle, looks up and meets her eye, lets her know he approves, that he wants to be hers. And back in the truck, the dog watches the road ahead as vigilantly as though he were driving himself, yet every so often he looks behind, just to be sure.

bert

Al Murdoch watches the girl as she fastens the collar around her dog's neck. The dog wags his tail, accepts the symbol of ownership, races once around the forecourt before leaping back inside the truck.

Al smiles to himself. He'd kept Bert's collar all these months, held it sometimes, running his fingers along the webbing, trying to recapture the scent of the dog on his fingers.

Yet he knows it's time to let go, that the collar has found a good home. Sometimes it made him feel worse when he saw it there under the shop counter, reminding him of the accident, of the blood in the dirt. Bert looked so perfect, as though the car had hardly touched him, as though he were sleeping, yet when Al got up close he'd seen the darkening ribbon of blood trickling from his mouth.

And what about the girl? He knows she's running from something bad, from that used car salesman up at Oakridge by the looks of the truck. She must be the daughter of that woman from the coast he took up with recently. No one thought it would last long, not with his reputation for liking the younger girls. And from the gossip he's heard over the years, this one isn't the first to do a runner from Sherman Rook. Yet she's different to most of them – this girl still has something innocent about her, as though she got away before the damage was done. And this girl has her dog. Hal, she says she calls him.

Al had watched the dog through the window

when they first pulled up, saw him waiting for the girl; a skinny thing, red as a fox, with a blaze of white across his chest. He became restless when the girl went out of sight, trotting back and forth, stirring up the dust, his tongue lolling, head on one side, always alert. Al could see he was a young dog, that his teeth were white and strong, his eyes bright with something you might call love.

And now, as they turn around in the forecourt, he can see the dark profile of the dog's head through the open window, the blonde head of the girl, and he suddenly feels the weight of his loss like a punch in the gut. He pulls out a photo of Bert that was stuck down the side of the till; Bert when he was scarcely more than a puppy, legs too long for his body, his face a daft grin. Al's wife, Maddie, standing above the creek, shielding her eyes from the sun, a cigarette between her fingers, a thin trail of smoke floating above her head like a halo. Bert is looking up at her as if waiting for instructions, yet she's staring straight at the camera, straight at Al. He misses them both, ain't that a fact.

Al's happy he could help the girl, pleased she has the dog to protect her. With a little luck he knows they'll make it. When he looks up again they're out of sight, and he goes outside, kicks over the tyre marks in the dust, and later that day he wipes the security footage clean.

Just before closing time he flicks through the pile of mail on the counter, looking for the flyer from the local dog pound. At 6.30 sharp he locks the shop door and goes out to his truck. There's no dog to match Bert, he knows that, and no one can persuade him otherwise.

But he's willing to take a chance, and if he finds a dog he likes the look of he might just call him Hal.

frozen fish

Mollie keeps driving for longer than she'd intended, stops to check the map every so often, takes the winding back roads to avoid being seen. But eventually she realises they're taking her nowhere fast and she heads over to the highway again. The traffic is heavier now and she knows better than to drive much further. She sees the bright neon sign of a roadhouse a short way ahead and pulls off the road onto a narrow track, finds a place to park the pickup that's shaded by trees and out of sight of passing cars. She lays herself out across the seats for a while and when she wakes up the sun is low in the sky.

Mollie gets out to stretch her legs and Hal follows. There's an abandoned clapboard house hidden behind the trees, its roof half-missing, the screen door hanging from one hinge. She walks up the drive a little way to a small fish pond. In this perfect oasis, a stone's throw from the dirt of the highway, water lilies bloom in a tangle of weed, creamy and waxy, the petals washed with pink. She leans over, catches a glimpse of something orange and silver dart between the leaves.

She remembers that afternoon in the park two winters ago, the paths thick with snow. As she passed by the lily pond with Chrissy, they glimpsed a goldfish, a prisoner beneath thin ice. Mollie broke the surface with the heel of her boot, plunged a hand into the water, then clenched her fist for a moment, immobilised by an irrational fear of touching the glint and gleam of the fish.

She could still picture Pepper, her childhood

47

goldfish, thrashing on the kitchen counter. She forgot to put the lid back on the tank one day and he leapt to freedom. She called for her mama, tentatively holding her hand out towards the fish, already imagining the cold wriggle of him, the feel of his tiny heart pulsing, the possibility that he would slither from her grasp and land on the tiled floor.

Pepper's body gave a final jerk as her mama arrived in the room. She dropped him back into the tank, but he stayed on his side, floating among flakes of fish food, his mouth open in surprise.

They went into town later, bought Mollie new hair ribbons, ate strawberry sundaes at her favourite ice cream parlour. Yet it didn't help one bit.

Back home, they buried Pepper in the yard, and the following week Mollie chose a new fish from the pet store. He was silver and she called him Salt, but somehow he never overwrote the memory of Pepper, preferring instead to serve as a daily reminder that she'd allowed him to die.

And at the fish pond on that December afternoon, there'd been the opportunity for redemption, a chance to make amends. Despite her fear, Mollie reached for the fish, teeth gritted, felt him quivering as she scooped him up with a paper coffee cup. They carried him home carefully, Chrissy warming the cup in her mittened hands.

The goldfish spent winter in a borrowed bowl, and they admired his shimmer as he circled the pirate ship, wove through weed in a one-man glittering shoal, made eyes at the mermaid with the yellow plait.

In April they carried him back to the pond,

squatted down at the edge to watch him explore. But his tail flicked once and he was already gone, leaving only a ripple between the lily pads to say he was ever there, just as though he'd never known them.

Chrissy laughed, joked that he was one ungrateful fish, yet Mollie was simply happy to have rescued him; a life saved for a life lost. That was her reward – she had atoned for her mistake.

If only everything in life was as easy to put right as scooping a fish from a frozen pond. She wasn't there to save Chrissy from the creek, wasn't able to save her mama from Sherman Rook. She feels a stab of guilt for leaving Mama behind, for jumping out of the tank to take her chances, for following in her daddy's footsteps.

Mollie tries not to think about Chrissy too often, because then she doesn't have to accept her death. She still feels guilty for not being with her that night, is still unable to bear thinking about her waxen face in the open casket. She looks up at the sky for a moment, suddenly certain Chrissy is right there, that she can hear her voice telling Mollie to keep on going.

his name is star

A dog is tied up outside the Horseshoe Bar, a length of rope looped around his collar. His head is resting on his paws, but he's not asleep, he's simply resigned to waiting – for now at least. Jack can see the whites of his eyes in the dark. The dog's head goes up every time the door opens, then down again when it closes. Something about his shape looks familiar, even in the low light, and when he lifts his head there's a glimpse of white at his throat, a blaze that runs aslant across his chest.

How many miles were they from Stoneacre now – a hundred at least? Yet Jack reckons that's not so far for a dog to wander, and he's had a good few weeks to walk it.

When the bailiffs came, Star barked at them with a fury Jack hadn't known was within him. He bared his teeth, frothed at the mouth like some crazy wild coyote, even though he'd never so much as caught a cottontail or growled at the postman before. The men told Jack to keep the dog under control or they'd shoot, and he shut Star in the cab of his truck while he loaded the remains of their possessions into the back. But when his wife opened the door, the dog shot out like a greyhound from a trap, chased the bailiffs' wagon down the highway as fast as he could run. When Jack and his wife set off behind them he was sure they'd find Star waiting at the side of the road somewhere. Yet they never did.

The dog stands up, tail wagging, as two bikers come out of the bar, helmets tucked under their arms. His tail drops again when he sees they're not who he's waiting for, and they pat his head absentmindedly as they pass. Jack can make out the blaze on his chest now, narrow at the top, then widening and curving off to the right, like the trail of a shooting star in a child's drawing.

He swings out of the cab, pulls on his cap, then walks towards the door. The dog is lying down again, head resting back on his paws, and when Jack gets nearer he can see for sure it's Star, wearing a red collar he's never seen before, faded and frayed as though it once had a previous owner. Star catches his scent on the evening breeze, glances up, wags his tail, then looks back at the bar door. As Jack crouches down to him, the dog's face fills with confusion and he stares at the door again. The next time it opens, a blonde girl comes out wearing jeans and a plaid shirt, a red jumper tied around her shoulders that's the same colour as Star's coat. She's carrying a plastic tub filled with water. When she sees Jack, she pauses, and the dog looks back and forth between them, dips his head, paws the ground, whines a little.

Jack takes in the situation straight away, realises this girl thinks she's Star's owner now.

The dog nudges his hand, licks it quickly, looks up at him imploringly, wanting him to understand, needing him to give permission, waiting for a sign to say he can stay with the girl. Jack holds Star's head gently between his hands. He can see he loves him, it's written all over his face. He's a young dog, barely grown, yet his loyalty shines clear in his eyes, and Jack knows if he takes him by the collar he won't resist. But there's something else in his eyes too, and he can sense that Star wants to be with this girl.

The girl is unsure what to say or do, at a disadvantage while her hands are occupied with the container of water. Jack can see that uncertainty, the flush of her cheeks, as she places the tub on the ground.

'Hal?' she calls, and there's a slight tremor in her voice, almost as though she's guessed why Jack is there.

Jack stands up, his outstretched palms facing downward, as though gesturing silently to the dog, letting him know it's okay for him to stay right there.

'His name is Star,' Jack says softly.

'I'm sorry?'

'I was just saying what a mighty fine dog you've got there, miss.' He touches his cap and walks past her into the bar.

teeth

Behind the Horseshoe Bar a group of bikers sit around two picnic tables, faces illuminated by the green and pink neon sign, their beers almost finished, the remains of a spliff passed hurriedly from hand to hand. They watch a dog and a girl appear from the direction of the trees. The girl walks across to them with a beer crate balanced on her hip, bottles chinking. She places it down on one of the tables and offers the beer in payment for somewhere to sleep for the night. They look her up and down, the girls with suspicion, and two of them pull out a bottle each, check the label, then let it fall back into the crate with a thunk. The tallest of the girls nods to her.

'How have you got here? We're five miles from the nearest town. You sure can't have walked that far with a crate of beer?'

The others laugh.

Mollie shrugs. 'I had transport, but now I haven't.'

'Okay . . . what's your name?'

'Mollie.'

'Pleased to meet you, Mollie. I'm Ginny. Say, just how old are you anyway?'

Mollie hesitates. 'Sixteen?' she tries.

Ginny looks her up and down, shakes her head and smiles.

'Well you've got some front, Miss Mollie, or maybe you're just too darn trusting for your own good – you don't know us from the devil! But I guess I can give you a couch for the night if that's what you want.

We were just about to leave for a party at mine anyhow. Danny can bring you and your beer in his car – meet us out the front in ten minutes?'

Mollie nods, loops Hal's rope around the bench while she goes back inside to the restroom. There's no sign of the trucker from earlier; the tall man in a red cap she'd seen crouched down with Hal. There was something strange about that whole thing, something she couldn't put her finger on. The dog was so relaxed with him; the way they looked at each other would have made anyone presume they were old friends.

When she comes back outside the bikers are pulling away one by one. Ginny jumps astride an old Honda, chrome gleaming in the beam of Danny's headlights. She fastens her helmet and gives Mollie the thumbs up before kickstarting the engine.

Danny is waiting in his car, engine running, arm hanging out of the window, tan against his white T-shirt.

The breeze is cool on Mollie's face as they take the highway east, and the thrum of the engines surrounds her like a shield. Hal pushes his damp nose into her neck, whines a little.

'It's okay,' she tells him, though suddenly she's not so certain. If Hal isn't sure, then he's probably right. She clutches her knapsack, feels the reassuring crinkle of the $20 note in her jeans pocket.

Ginny's place is on the edge of town, the yard overgrown with long grass, some kind of half-wild rose bushes scattering petals along the length of the path. She has already thrown open the windows and doors, music is drifting out across the street. Ginny hands Mollie a beer and gestures to the bench on the porch.

'No need to tell me who you're running from,' she says, 'just as long as no one's about to turn up here looking for you.'

Mollie shakes her head. 'No, they won't do that.'

'Where are you heading next?'

'I'm heading to my family in New Jersey, but I haven't enough money for the bus ride. Do you know of any jobs round here? I've worked in a diner before.'

Ginny laughs. 'There's nothing much around here, kid. But if you seriously want to make a few bucks for the bus fare then there is one thing I can think of, and as you're young and fit I'm sure I can get you good money.'

She laughs again, winks, unsure if the girl understands her, but Mollie is already nodding.

'I'll do pretty much anything.'

'Wait here then – if you're sure? I know a guy inside who'll be willing to help you out.'

'Now?' Mollie is suddenly confused.

'No time like the present?' Ginny takes hold of Hal by the collar as she heads for the door. 'I'll look after the dog for you – he's safer in the kitchen.'

Mollie stays on the porch, finishes her beer and takes another, already feeling a buzz from the alcohol she isn't accustomed to drinking. She can't figure out what this work could be, or why she has to go right away. Cleaning up in a bar? Or maybe the late-night grocery store?

When Ginny comes back outside she's with a short bald guy who Mollie remembers from the Horseshoe Bar. He pulls her up from the bench without a word, a bunch of car keys jangling in his other hand. She grabs her knapsack and follows him.

As they walk around to the back of the house, Mollie can hear Hal barking, high-pitched and urgent. Something clicks inside her head and she knows she's made a mistake. The man opens the back door of a rusting station wagon and gestures for her to climb inside.

'Where are we going?' she asks.

'Going? We ain't going nowhere, lady. The action's right here.'

He laughs as he pushes her into the car. She can feel his fingers scrape the skin on her arm, rough as Sherman Rook's hands, can smell the stale sweat on him as she shies away from the hot stench of his breath. He shoves her head down towards his crotch as he starts to unfasten his jeans.

For a moment Mollie is paralysed by fear, stunned by her own stupidity, yet she can already feel it hardening into rage. She knows she can't let this happen, isn't prepared for her journey to end this way.

She lunges across, grabs the door handle and kicks it open, but he still has hold of her other arm. She swings back her free arm and punches him as hard as she can, feels her knuckle crunch against his cheek. Above his angry grunt she hears a low growl and the skitter of claws across the yard. She watches the man's face change when a set of strong white teeth sink into his flesh. For a moment he loosens his grip on her shoulder and she pushes her way out of the door, rolling over in the dust until she feels Hal's tongue licking her hand. She jumps up and swings over the low fence into the neighbour's yard, crouches down beyond the trees and pulls the dog behind her.

She hears him slam his fist on the roof of the car, then shout for Ginny, and when she peers out he is looking up and down the street. Eventually he shrugs and heads round to the house. When Mollie jumps back over the fence she sees a trickle of blood turning black in the dust.

guinea pigs can die of loneliness

The bus station is quiet at 4 a.m. and the ticket office is closed. Mollie is still unsure whether to spend her money on a bus ticket, but for now it's a good place to rest for a while and plan what to do. She lies out of sight on one of the wooden benches at the back, and Hal sits on the floor at her side, his head resting on her feet. His eyes are open, his ears are cocked, tuned in to every sound out on the street.

Mollie stares up at the high glass roof, watches the sky lighten, sees the ghostly shapes of birds through dirty green panes, the outlines of their delicate feet as they criss-cross the glass. She listens to the small noises: the faint tap of the birds' claws, the gentle burbling of the collared dove huddled in the rafters, the scrape of a candy wrapper scuttling across the floor when the breeze blows through the open door. She sits up cautiously when she hears heavy footsteps.

A man comes into view, his boot cleats scraping the tiles as he crosses to the bench opposite Mollie's. He places a small wooden box on the seat beside him. Through the wire mesh Mollie can make out a black and white guinea pig.

When Mollie was eight years old she'd begged her mother to let her have a guinea pig.

'But you have a rabbit and a goldfish already. You never clean out the fish – no wonder the last one jumped ship – and I struggle to get you to remember to feed Thumps.'

'I'll remember, Mama, I promise,' she said. 'The

61

guinea pig can live with Thumps in the same hutch – I checked in a book at the library. So they'll have each other for company, and all it will cost is a little extra food.'

She named the guinea pig Whiskey, and every day for the first few weeks she took him out of the hutch and combed him, brought him into the house, followed him round with a dustpan. She bathed him in the kitchen tub, wrapped him in the frayed pink towel her mama used as a duster, rubbed the long wet fur on his pot belly until he was dry again. Yet not long after that, her friend Franny got herself a tank of terrapins and Mollie forgot all about Whiskey.

A few months later, Thumps died of old age. For a week or so afterwards, Mollie took an interest in Whiskey again, fetched him back into the house and let him have the run of the den. Then Matty Marsden got a chocolate Labrador and the guinea pig took a back seat once more.

One morning at breakfast, Mama told her Whiskey had died the night before.

'You know, Mollie, guinea pigs can die of loneliness.'

She opened her eyes wide. 'Loneliness? But he had us.'

Her mama shook her head. 'When was the last time you picked him up or talked to him? I read somewhere that it's best to keep a minimum of two guinea pigs. It should be compulsory really – there needs to be a law like that for humans too.'

Her mama laughed, but Mollie could see she was sad. She got up from the table and went over to her. She wrapped one arm around her waist and reached for her brother with the other.

'Well the three of us have got each other, so we're okay?'

Her mama brushed Mollie's hair back from her face, lifted up her chin with her finger and placed a kiss on her nose.

'We sure have, sweetie, and we sure are okay.'

But even as she said it, Mollie knew it wasn't true, was scared her mother might die of loneliness too. She watched her gaze out of the window to where the road curved away.

Her mother sometimes paced back and forth along the length of the porch after Mollie and Angel had gone to bed. Even though she wore soft shoes, Mollie could hear her footsteps through the open window, the clearing of her throat, the rustle of her skirt. She knew her mother was still waiting, still hoping for her daddy to return.

Mama loved to tell anyone who'd listen that everyone leaves her in the end. Now Mollie has left her too.

She stands up, goes over to the man with the guinea pig, pushes her finger through the chicken wire that covers the front of the box.

'Careful she doesn't bite,' he says. 'I'm taking her home to be a companion to my other two. I saw her on her own in the pet store and I couldn't bear the idea of her being all alone out in somebody's yard.'

'Does she have a name?'

He shakes his head.

'You could call her Ella, after my mama?'

The man lifts up the box and looks at her. 'Ella,' he repeats. 'Yes, I like that.'

tiger

Mollie stands at the roadside with her homemade sign.

"Anywhere – Jersey shore" with "Thank You" in large letters underneath. She's made a smaller one for Hal and persuaded him to hold it in his mouth so he looks cute and friendly.

A woman stops in a red Corolla, her daughter sitting up front with her, a frail-looking girl with wide, dark eyes.

'Can take you as far as the next town,' she says. 'Bankstone, just across the county line.'

Mollie nods and thanks her, grateful for a lift of any length. They've been waiting there almost two hours.

She climbs in the back behind the daughter, pushes Hal down low on the seat. The girl is holding a small Kodak camera on her lap. She turns towards them, leans into the gap between the seats and takes a photo of them both without saying a word. When she lowers the camera, she stares straight through Mollie and out of the back window, her eyes unblinking, face as pale as a ghost.

For a split second she looks exactly like Michelle.

Michelle turned up at the start of fourth grade. Everyone thought she was special. She was freckled and fragile as a sparrow's egg, her bones as brittle as brandy snap, skin so pale it was almost blue, as though they were all watching her underwater.

Evelyn told Mollie it was Michelle's heart

that didn't work properly. Sometimes it went too fast, sometimes it missed a beat or two, and one day it might fizz and pop. In the summer vacation, Mollie wanted to go swimming, play outdoors, cycle over to the forest, just like they always did, but Evelyn and Franny were happy to play inside with Michelle every afternoon.

Michelle's mother never let her play outside, but she didn't seem to care. She didn't need outdoors. She'd slide inside Mollie's mama's old coney coat, prowl and purr along the hallway, make-believe claws clicking on the wood. They'd laugh and squeal as she lunged towards them, tiger-fierce, all hiss and roar and mothball-scented growl. They climbed up the stairs behind her on their hands and knees, the thick carpet lush as snow as they conquered Everest. Michelle was their expedition leader, carrying a torn sandcastle flag to the summit.

Then one afternoon Michelle stopped by Mollie's house after school and they went into the yard to play. Evelyn and Franny said they shouldn't, but Mollie's mama was working in the diner and there was no one to stop them. Mollie told Michelle that if she were a real tiger she'd climb up to the second branch of the tree with her. Michelle just smiled and scrambled up without a murmur, her knees cracking like gunshot, and when they were seated side by side on the wide, flat branch, the others called up to her and told her to be careful.

It was right there and then, listening to the rattle and wheeze of Michelle's breath, that Mollie decided she couldn't bear her being special a moment longer. She hated her clever worlds of make-believe, her yellow pinafore dress that never got dirty, her fierce yet fragile heart; she was jealous of her smile that lit up the world.

And when no one was watching, Mollie pushed.

There was a thud, a strange silence, her lathe-thin body crumpled in the dust, limbs at awkward angles. Then the wail of the siren, the flashing lights, Evelyn's mouth in a perfect O, Michelle's mother howling in the ambulance.

When they were told she wasn't coming home for a long time, Mollie pressed her face into the dusty pelts of her mama's coat and whispered a prayer: she offered to make a deal with Jesus. He could take her ballerina music box and her shells if he'd turn Mama's coat back into a tiger. She hadn't meant to hurt Michelle, she truly hadn't. She was just jealous for a moment and forgot how high up they were. But her words were swallowed by soft fur and Jesus didn't hear them. When Michelle came out of hospital she never came back to school and the family moved away soon afterwards.

Mollie stares straight back at the girl in the car and smiles, but the child's face remains expressionless. A shiver runs through her; it's as though she can read her thoughts, as though she's Michelle's doppelgänger sent to remind her of what she did.

'I like your dog,' the girl says quietly. She reaches through the gap in the seats and strokes Hal's head for a few moments, then turns back round, watching the road ahead in silence.

When they get out of the car at Bankstone, the girl lifts up the Kodak again and takes a photo of Mollie and Hal standing at the side of the road. Then she lowers the camera and watches them as they wait for the traffic to clear. As the car pulls away, Mollie swears she sees the ghost of Michelle's smile playing around the girl's lips, and for some inexplicable reason she feels forgiven.

still waters

Phil Archer's family home had been noisy and sometimes fractious, yet always full of love.

His brother played the drums, the tap and pound and crash of them thumping through the floor above Phil's bedroom, and his sister was in a girls' choir organised by his mother. The choir used to meet at their house every Tuesday evening. He wouldn't have minded so much if they'd been older girls, but his sister was five years his junior. They squealed and giggled, ran along the corridor like elephants, went all shy and coy when he passed them on the porch steps.

His father wasn't musical, but he made his own noise. He created furniture from salvaged wood, put up shelves in the den, redesigned the garden, tiled the bathroom. Every day they'd hear the vibration of his drill through the walls, the sound of a hammer, a sander, a planer. The house was always filled with the smell of varnish and wood shavings.

Phil had never craved attention. At school he was quiet yet popular, sporty but not a team captain, clever but never top of the class. He found the boys in his class too arrogant and loud, the girls too pushy and shrill. And at home, all he craved was a piece of quiet time for himself, a few moments of solitude to clear his mind.

When it got too much he'd head down to his Uncle Sonny's boatyard beyond the end of the boardwalk, sit quietly in the corner listening to him whistle softly as he worked. There was hammering and sanding here too, the distant crash of the waves, yet this noise didn't bother Phil at all. There was a measured calm in it, a simple sense of purpose. A country channel played on the radio in the background, and there was a quiet companionship between nephew and uncle that anchored Phil, that made him feel useful and needed.

His uncle was a single man, a confirmed bachelor, and he told Phil he would be happy to give him a job there when he left school, so he could attend the local college one day a week, learn carpentry and nautical studies, and when his uncle retired he could take over the business. His parents thought it was a throwaway offer, that Phil would grow out of the idea, that Sonny wasn't serious. Yet Phil already knew for certain exactly what he wanted to do when he grew up and he never changed his mind. As soon as he left school he went down to the boatyard and started working for his uncle.

Janet Pearlman had hair as glossy as a newly split chestnut and she wore it coiled around her head in a thick plait. Phil had seen her surfing on her own when he was down at the boatyard, had admired her taut stomach, her long legs, had noticed how she swam as strongly as the boys. He caught her scent when she brushed past him in the soda shop, sharp and fresh as lemons.

She was different from the other girls. They let their hair hang loose, and each of them wore the same cheap floral perfume from the drug store and painted their nails a uniform oyster pink. They giggled and chattered, all of a flutter, whispered behind their hands.

Janet had an air of surety, of quiet confidence

and poise. There was nothing brash or loud about her, she was calm and cool and clear; a pool of still water. And Phil Archer knew still waters ran deep.

He'd watched her for weeks, had wanted to ask her out, but hadn't yet plucked up the courage. He knew she was a little younger than him – perhaps seventeen. He'd smiled at her across the soda shop, made small talk at the counter when her friend went to the restroom. Now he studied her at the jukebox, making her choices with quiet consideration, never turning to her friends for input or reassurance. Her right hand was resting on the glass, the slender index finger of her left hand running down the columns of songs, reading the handwritten labels carefully, as though she hadn't seen them all a hundred times before.

Some of the boys stood up, got ready to leave, fastened their leather jackets and retrieved their helmets. Phil took his chance while everyone was distracted, jumped up quickly and approached Janet at the jukebox.

'Would you like to come out for a ride with me?' he asked.

She nodded and went back over to the counter, whispered something to her friend. Phil handed her one of the spare helmets from behind the door, and she fastened her Levi jacket, followed him out onto the street without a word.

As they took the first corner she leaned outwards instead of into the bend, and he realised she'd never ridden pillion before. He slowed down, twisted round and shouted to her.

'You need to lean with me into the bends! It's okay, you won't fall off – keep tight hold of me.'

He felt her arms slide around him, her hands slip into his pockets, the side of her helmet rest gently against his back.

When they reached the pine woods he turned down a dirt track, wound slowly through the trees until they reached a picnic bench at the end. He took Janet's hand and led her to the viewpoint, the moonlight illuminating her skin. She gasped when she realised they were standing on top of a hillside, the night sky wide open above them.

He spread out his jacket on the carpet of dry pine needles at the edge of the trees, and she lay down with him, hesitant at first, both of them listening to the small noises in the forest and the sound of their own breathing. He had only intended to kiss her, but when Janet unfastened the button of his jeans, slid her fingers beneath the waistband, it felt as though she'd planned it all along. When he slipped his hand inside the soft cotton of her shirt, she didn't miss a beat, didn't hesitate, gave herself to him without a murmur, holding his head between her hands as he pushed inside her.

They dressed again in silence, suddenly shy. As she fastened the strap of her helmet she turned to him and smiled. 'That was my first time,' she said.

'Mine too,' he said quickly.

'You don't have to pretend just to make me feel better. I wanted you to know, that's all. My family are moving to Longfield next week, down near Atlantic City – that's why I said yes tonight. I can't explain why, but I knew I wanted you to be the first, even though we won't see each other again.'

He moved towards her then, reached beneath

her chin to unfasten the helmet, then placed it over the handlebars and led her back to the trees.

Phil meant to go and visit Janet once she'd moved down to Longfield, but three weeks later he met Ella Jones.

She had just turned eighteen, yet she dressed like a woman rather than a girl, wore swept-up eyeliner and pink twinsets that hugged her full breasts. Her hair was always piled up high. Ella was a man's woman, but Phil wasn't worldly enough to recognise the signs. He couldn't see that she dressed to tempt, to lure her catch, to snare potential husbands. She was pretty in her own way, but it was a fragile beauty. There was something transient about it, something brittle, something easily broken. Ella had her own kind of confidence, yet it was little more than a trick, a show, an act. She flirted shamelessly with everyone, all vermillion lips and frosted nails, all pout and smile and hands on hips, all thrust and come-on. She knew what she wanted and she meant to get it.

Ella sucked Phil into her whirlpool. There were to be no still waters.

mud snail shells

Saul Bradshaw is sitting in a lane not far from the Horseshoe Bar. He's been sent there to collect his boss's pickup, yet although he was dropped off first thing with the spare key, some twenty minutes later he hasn't even stuck it in the ignition.

Sly told him the story on the way over. It was Mollie Archer, the boss's so-called stepdaughter, who'd stolen the truck from under his nose and driven it as far as here. It might have stayed hidden beneath the trees for weeks, but a farmer reported it to the cops when he couldn't get his tractor through.

The story is that after the girl abandoned it there she carried on east, back to the Jersey shore – hitching rides they presume – but no one knows for sure. Sly says the boss doesn't like to talk about it much.

Saul has only seen Mollie the once, that time Sherman Rook sent him over to Oakridge Farm to swap two tyres on his station wagon. She sat on the porch and watched him, but it didn't seem like she wanted to make conversation. He remembers her face, that soft skin like peaches and cream, her long legs stretched out in the sun. She had a look about her that he liked; something in her dark eyes both fearful and strong.

The pickup holds no clues; the glovebox is empty and there's nothing much in the back. Saul pulls down the visor and another set of keys falls straight into his lap. He jumps, even though he was already half-expecting to find them there.

That's when he sees it – something glinting in

the passenger footwell. He reaches down and picks it up. A shell. A mud snail shell that's travelled a clear thousand miles or more from the shore. He holds it up to the light, a ridged whorl of gold.

In all his nineteen years he's only made one trip to the shore.

It was the time his mother took him to stay with his aunt and uncle when he was six or seven years old. Back then, before his daddy left, they lived further east and could get to his aunt's in four or five hours on the bus. Jenny was just twenty miles inland from Atlantic City, and Uncle Pete drove them all down to the boardwalk one morning.

When Saul caught his first glimpse of the sea he pointed in excitement, turned to the others, eyes shining.

'The sea! The sea!' he shouted.

His Aunty Jenny and Uncle Pete laughed, touched by the boy's enthusiasm, yet his mother didn't even raise a smile. Uncle Pete bought them ice cream sodas and chilli dogs, set down an old check picnic rug on the sand.

His mother had been snappy that day, told his aunt and uncle they were spoiling him, that he wouldn't eat his dinner later. Aunty Jenny reached for her hand, said she knew it was hard for her right now, but the boy needed a break too. Saul didn't understand why it was hard for his mother right then, didn't yet know about his daddy and Maria with the silver Chevrolet. He looked up at her to see how she would reply, yet she just shook her hand free and nodded. When they went down to the dunes she stayed up on the boardwalk, clutching her pack of cigarettes close to her chest as she gazed out at the ocean.

Saul kicked off his plimsolls, ran straight down to the water, his feet burning in the hot sand, clutching the faded hand-me-down bucket that had belonged to his cousin. He zigzagged between the deckchairs and the windbreaks, picked up a piece of driftwood and threw it into the waves, watched the ocean pull it away and then hurl it onto the sand again.

He threw back his head and watched the gulls circling overhead on the thermals, smelt the dank seaweed stranded by the tide, then plunged into the shallows, his trousers rolled up to the knee, not caring if he got wet. When he tired of the waves he walked along the firm strip of beach at the water's edge, still damp from the receding tide. And there they were, the spoils of the sea: emerald sea glass, striped coquinas, golden mud snail shells, glinting like treasure in the sand. He picked them all up, one by one, marvelling at each shell before he dropped it gently into the bucket, imagining them lined up on his window ledge at home. He raced back up the beach to show his aunt and uncle, and it was then he heard his mother calling him from the boardwalk. She leaned heavily on the railings, the nub of a cigarette held between her finger and thumb.

'What you got there, Saul?'

He ran up the steps to show her, picked out the two most beautiful of the striped coquinas, then placed them side by side on the railing. They were as pale as the sand, their insides a dark purple that reminded him of Mama's best velvet dress.

'These are for you, Mama,' he said.

She glanced down at the shells, grunted her

thanks, and put them in her pocket without a second glance.

'And you can forget it if you think you're bringing that load of junk all the way home with you.'

She held out her hand for the bucket, but he tucked it behind his back.

'I can leave them in Aunty Jenny's garden until next time,' he said. 'She won't mind, I know she won't.'

His mother reached around his back and pulled the bucket from his hands, spilling the contents across the planks of the boardwalk.

'No!' she shouted. 'You'll do as I say!'

She stamped her foot and smashed the prettiest of the mud snail shells clean in two.

And now, in this pickup truck, he's found a shell that's even prettier. He reckons this girl who took the truck from Sherman Rook's place must have been hankering after the shore too, clinging to her memories as fiercely as he holds on to his own. He slips the shell in his pocket before he sticks the pickup into reverse. One day soon he might get back there, and if he finds her he'll just hold out the mud snail in the palm of his hand. He won't need any words.

soft

Sherman Rook has his feet up on the desk, is almost dozing off after his lunchtime beer at Lily Brown's. He thinks about Joanna, the pretty new barmaid he's working on, wonders if she'd be game for a threesome with Candice or Sue. He never pays for any of Lily's girls, he simply switches on the charm and promises them presents. He jerks awake as he hears the crunch of gravel on the forecourt, looks up to see Saul Bradshaw stepping down from the old Ford truck.

Sherman picks up his hat and steps outside, takes a walk round the pickup and kicks each tyre in turn.

'She looks okay to me,' he says, nodding. 'You find anything in the cab?'

Saul shakes his head, closes his hand around the mud snail shell in his pocket, traces the whorls with his finger.

Sherman holds out his hand for the keys, looks the boy up and down. He thinks about the new barmaid again, wonders if he should go back over to Lily's. He knows it won't be long before Joanna will be following him up the stairs to his usual room, and he allows himself to imagine her kneeling down in front of him.

Getting the truck back in one piece has eased his mind too, made him feel uncharacteristically magnanimous.

'You can look after the office for me this afternoon, Saul. Sly's out on a job with Stevie. Just call me over at Lily's if there's anything urgent – I think I'll take a walk down there and come back for the truck later.'

Saul nods. He knows that means Sherman Rook will be staying over at Lily Brown's for the night.

'Oh, and Saul?'

'Yes, Mr Rook?'

'You can take next week off – have yourself a vacation.'

'But Mr Rook, you and Sly are going down south for that car next week, who'll look after the office?'

Sherman pauses a moment; he hadn't thought of that.

'It'll be fine, Saul, just fine. I'm sure Stevie can cope. Take the week off – treat yourself!'

Sherman Rook feels something he's not too familiar with as he walks down Main Street. He feels pleased with himself for being kind to a fellow human being, for making Saul Bradshaw happy. Seeing the boy's face light up has somehow made everything right in the world.

He laughs to himself – he mustn't go soft in his old age, that would never do at all.

The only fly in his ointment is Ella Archer, brooding and sulking up at the farm all the while, making life miserable. Why did she have to turn out like all the others?

It had been good at the start; she'd had a smile as wide as her face, a pretty dimple in her left cheek, something both feisty and accommodating about her that he liked. He might even admit he'd been bowled over by her, that he was very fond of her at first.

But then Ella changed, almost overnight. It

was though Oakridge had sucked the life from her and turned her into his own mama.

His mother had been a vivacious and cheerful woman when she was younger, but she was eventually browbeaten by his pa, giving in to everything for a quiet life. When Sherman was a boy he'd silently willed her to stand up to his bullying father, yet she'd always remained quiet, letting her son suffer endless thrashings for little or nothing, taking her own beatings without a word. Sherman had often listened at their bedroom door, heard his pa's grunts as the belt swished, but there was never a single sound from his mama.

Now his own house is turning out to be exactly the same. That goddam Ella Archer is driving him to behave just as his daddy once did. History is slowly repeating itself. He'd vowed to give up Lily's and all the girls when he first brought Ella and Mollie home to Oakridge. He was sure they'd save him, make him turn over a new leaf. But he didn't have the willpower to break free of his old habits, and now he finds himself spending more time over at the bar than ever.

He could see Ella was homesick at the start, a little sad at leaving her friends and her old life behind. He knew he should have said the right things, reassured her that he'd look after her, that she'd make new friends. But he couldn't get the words out – playing all gentle with a woman was a sign of weakness and no mistake. If he'd shown his soft underbelly, who knows what advantage she'd have taken. Then there was that day when she showed him up by walking into Lily's with the girl. Unforgivable.

And now, the quieter and more compliant she

becomes, the more he feels the need to hurt her, to beat her, just as his pa beat his mama. Can't she see that all he wants is a reaction?

He reminds himself that she's still a useful housekeeper – and at least he's well rid of that miserable daughter of hers. She ended up causing him nothing but trouble, slinking around like her mother, never smiling, tempting him with her long limbs while locking her door to him.

And she made him a laughing stock by stealing his pickup truck.

He thumps his fist against a mailbox as he passes, can feel his good mood evaporating. Then he thinks about Joanna's full breasts, her red lips, about his trip away the following week, and everything is right in his world again. He won't let Ella Archer spoil a single damn thing.

chasing boys

Mollie was never good at keeping friends. There'd been Franny and Evelyn at elementary school, but they closed ranks after all the fuss about Michelle, stopped asking her over, never called round. She didn't really miss them until after her daddy left home, having always preferred to be with him down at the boatyard, combing the beach all summer, painting her shells and pebbles with yacht varnish to keep the colours bright, sitting in the yard office by the stove in winter. She'd take out her school books and work through her homework while she listened to the rhythmic sounds of her daddy sanding and sawing, painting and hammering, waiting impatiently for him to come through to see what she was doing, to ruffle her hair and say, 'How's my very best girl?'

At the start of junior high everyone already knew each other, and when all the desks had been chosen, rejected, squabbled over, Mollie found herself alone near the front of the class. Eventually Miss Draper brought a girl over to sit at the next desk and introduced her as Chrissy.

Chrissy Lawrence was new in town. Her father had recently been posted to New Jersey from his office in Philadelphia, and from the moment she was allocated the desk, Mollie knew they'd be friends. The girls were both daydreamers and they spent hours together in Chrissy's bedroom planning their perfect futures in New York City. They imagined sharing a SoHo apartment, painting the floorboards black and white, fashioning bookshelves from orange crates, hanging framed movie posters on the walls. They'd get jobs together in one of the fancy department stores, or in stylish offices where they could chat and drink coffee all day, and in the evenings they'd go out to downtown bars and clubs.

In their breaks at school they read comic strip romances in teen magazines, cut out pictures of Robert Redford and James Taylor to stick inside their locker doors. On Saturdays they bought cheap lipsticks and eye palettes from the dime store, practised creating their New York look in Chrissy's vanity mirror. In the early evenings they sat in the window at Pacitto's ice cream parlour, made a milkshake last two hours as they watched the boys promenade up and down the boardwalk.

In the last week of August, the year they turned thirteen, they sat on the boardwalk railings and listened to the rattle and clack of the rollercoaster, the screams and laughter from the dodgems. They'd soon be back in school, dreams cut down to size as summer came to a close. They watched the sky turn to fire as the sun disappeared behind the Cascade dance hall, and their future came so close that Mollie could almost touch it. For a few seconds the amusement park fell silent, the crash and roar of the Atlantic Ocean receded. The waves that lapped the beach were suddenly from a gentler sea. Mollie could picture a tropical island where the air was full of the scent of jasmine and frangipani, where music drifted out from a distant bar and couples danced together on the moonlit sand.

Chrissy's eyes met hers and there was a split second of recognition, as though they'd had the same vision but both knew it was a lie. In that strange, unnatural quiet there'd been a moment when they'd dared to believe that life would be special – a riot of colour and gloss and sparkle. But Mollie could see something dark below the glittering surface, could feel a tightness in her chest, the same tightness she felt when she watched Janet Pearlman reach for her daddy's hand. They both jumped down from the railings without saying a word, walked home in silence under a full moon, too scared to voice their fears and doubts.

They spent the following summer chasing boys, idling away their vacation in the boardwalk arcades. They painted their toenails cobalt blue, practised fixing false eyelashes, frayed the bottoms of their jeans and tied long Indian scarves around their heads. They had just turned fourteen and they thought they were all grown-up. They snapped gum and blew smoke rings in front of the corner boys who were waiting for their lives to begin. The boys knew Mollie and Chrissy were jail bait, yet they still let them act out with them, revelling in the attention as they admired their own reflections and rolled up their shirt sleeves to reveal new tattoos. Two of the boys found summer jobs in the pizza take-out, served the girls with free slices of Margherita, were rewarded with shy smiles and promises of making out under the boardwalk after closing time.

But the girls were too scared to follow through on those promises quite yet. It was only a trial, a practice run, just like smoking without inhaling. They looked the part but they weren't ready for the action. They were wading just out of their depth, learning to strut and flirt and pose, casting a net for a catch they weren't ready to haul in.

And when they'd tired of the boardwalk boys, the wannabe pool hustlers and the tourists, they pursued the boys who met up in the Tomato Dip. They'd drive through the Pine Barrens with Sam and Tony and Ronnie, piling into the back of Davey's pickup, racing along forest tracks with the wind ripping through their hair, Mollie and Chrissy squashed in together, their backs against the cab where they felt the safest. The boys turned up the radio as loud as they could, drowning out the girls' screams, driving over the bumps in the tracks as fast as they dared, laughing when the girls were thrown into the air, their knuckles as white as their faces as they gripped the sides of the truck. At every bend there was a moment when the pickup might leave the track and hurtle headlong into a tree, might turn turtle into the ditch. But no one seemed to care; adrenaline and pure joy pumped through their veins, and their screams were snatched away by the warm evening air. They were in a movie, an alternative reality, where no harm could befall them, where bad things only happened to other people, and although they boasted they were too fast to live, they held on to the certainty they were invincible.

One Saturday night in October, when the roads were wet and strewn with leaves, it turned out that Sam Madden was much too fast to live after all. Mollie was away that weekend, down in Longfield visiting her daddy, and Chrissy decided to go out without her, even though she'd sworn she wouldn't. When Sam came over to her table in Pacitto's and asked if she wanted to go for a drive, she knew she should say no. Sam Madden was seventeen, Chrissy barely fourteen, plus it was already late and her mama would be expecting her home. Not to mention that Mollie was sweet on Sam and would never forgive her.

Yet when his car clipped a tree root on a bend, Chrissy Lawrence was in the passenger seat holding his hand. The car bounced and somersaulted before landing upside down in the creek, and it was two days later when their bodies were found.

joanna

Joanna Crawford has worked at Lily Brown's for two weeks. She's a pretty girl, yet she hasn't quite realised it yet. She notices the way men look at her across the bar, the way their eyes follow her when she walks around the room collecting glasses. She stands in front of the full-length mirror in her room and appraises what she sees, a little unsure about her pale complexion, the scattering of freckles across her nose, her mane of unruly hair the colour of warm marmalade. Yet when she lifts up her shirt and twists and turns in front of the glass, she can find no fault with her full breasts and her taut, flat stomach. Satisfied, she goes down to the bar and turns on her sweetest smile.

Joanna was working in a burger joint somewhere in Indiana before she came to Lily's, but had been forced to leave there in a hurry on account of her roommate jumping ship without having paid the rent for four months. It was Joanna's first house share since leaving home. She'd answered an advert in the grocery store, hoping to make a new friend as well as finding a place to live. But Wendy worked shifts in a laundry and their paths rarely crossed. On the 25th of every month, Joanna handed over her share of the rent, unaware that her roommate was conveniently forgetting to pass it on to the landlord.

When she realised Wendy had gone, Joanna didn't hang around waiting for the eviction notice. She packed up her rucksack and jumped on the next bus west.

A man sat himself down next to her after the second comfort stop, introduced himself as Allen, and they struck up a conversation as the highway rolled by in a cloud of dust. When Allen heard Joanna's story he told her about Lily Brown's place, a bar in some one-trick town she'd never heard of before. He told her Lily was hiring right now and she could get herself a room there too. Joanna thought it sounded a little like a wild west whorehouse, but Allen just laughed.

'Well I guess every bar is a kind of brothel one way or another,' he said. 'Wherever you go you'll find folk getting to know each other and exchanging sex for something – a place to live, a couple of drinks, someone to love them or make them feel better for a few hours.'

Joanna didn't know how to answer, wasn't sure what to make of him.

'I can introduce you if that helps? Put a word in? Lily and I, we go way back.'

'I'll think about it,' she said.

'Well don't think too long or too hard. Oakridge is the next stop, so I reckon you've got about twenty minutes to decide.'

As Joanna walks down the open staircase, she sees Sherman Rook is back. He turns to look up at her as though he's sensed her presence. She smiles, lifts her hand and waves. She's sure he's really sweet on her, but she hasn't decided what to do about it yet. She's asked the other girls about him, but they've said very little. He has a girlfriend who lives up at his farm, but no one ever sees her, and Candice says she's heard talk he's already on the lookout for a replacement.

Joanna studies him as she walks across to the bar. He's the urban cowboy type, all flashy buckles and polished toe rands. But she kind of likes that. When he smiles he's quite attractive, yet there's a strange coldness in his grey eyes that she can't weigh up, at odds with how friendly he appears. He leaves generous tips and buys her endless drinks, kisses her cheek each evening before he leaves. He takes her hand in both of his, looks her in the eye, tells her she's a real pretty girl, that she puts him in mind of someone. He says he can't remember who – some film star maybe, or a country singer.

Joanna is still struggling to work him out. She can see he isn't shy, but maybe he's a little cautious, maybe he's been taken for a ride by women before, or maybe he's simply flirting and isn't looking for a new girlfriend at all.

He stands at the bar waiting for her, orders a beer and a bourbon chaser, asks her to bring them over to a table in the corner. When she puts them down in front of him he grasps her wrist, asks her to sit with him for a while. Joanna looks back over to the end of the bar. Lily sits in a shaft of afternoon sunlight on a high stool, her brash blonde hair fixed up in a bun, a pack of cigarettes and a beer on the bar top.

'I'll have to ask Lily,' she says.

'She'll be fine, I'll square it with her.'

He shouts across, asks Lily if she can spare her prettiest barmaid for half an hour.

She nods, but when Joanna goes back across to the bar to fetch herself a drink, Lily pulls her to one side for a moment.

'This isn't a whorehouse, Joanna. I'm all for

keeping the customers sweet, but you do it in your own time and you don't take a dollar in return – I can't afford to have a visit from the law. Understand?'

'It's really nothing like that, Lily. What do you take me for?'

Lily laughs; a harsh, throaty laugh that says she doesn't believe a word of it.

'Sherman will see you right – buy you a pretty scarf and some dainty ear-bobs I dare say – but he soon gets bored, and he isn't a man to trifle with.'

Joanna takes a long swig of her beer, walks back over to the corner table, her heels clicking on the wooden floor. Sherman pats the seat next to him.

'Sit right down and tell me all about yourself,' he says.

one more chance

Mollie stands at the roadside for a little over an hour waiting for a ride. A few cars slow down, speeding up again when they see she's with a dog. A couple in a Plymouth almost stop, but when the wife realises how young and pretty Mollie is, she turns to her husband and tells him to drive on, her mouth all screwed up with jealousy.

Eventually a couple stop in a beat-up white Buick. They are in their late forties or early fifties, weatherworn, their style a touch old-fashioned. Mollie imagines them to be farmers, though their cheap town clothes suggest otherwise. Their accent is mid-west – though they say very little at all – and their faces are drawn, pale, blank as stone. They barely glance up as she climbs in the back with the dog at her side.

As they set off, the woman turns to Mollie, twists her thin shoulders round to face her full on. She stares in silence for a moment, her two small eyes shiny as beads.

'No talking on the journey. Father and I don't hold with talking. If you talk, you get out.'

Mollie nods, touches Hal's head as he lets out the whisper of a whine.

A Rhett Hewson song is playing on the radio. Mollie remembers her daddy buying this one from a secondhand vinyl store back when she was barely in school. She learned the lyrics that very same afternoon.

She has an urge to sing, but she bites back the words, mouthing them at the window as the blacktop streams past in a smooth black river. When the song finishes, Mollie wants to ask the name of the station they're listening to, leans forward to check which frequency the dial is turned to, yet she can't quite make it out. The woman's head turns, her nose as sharp as her eyes, and Mollie leans back against the seat and rests her arm across Hal's back.

The next song is something she doesn't know, but it's good. The singer's voice is dark as dusk, sometimes silk, sometimes rough as bark. He's lost his job, his money, his wife.

'. . . You let the screen door slam on our love, you were so quick to leave, you never did believe . . .'

She taps her hand gently on Hal's side.

They pass through a small town, are stopped by a set of lights just as the weather changes. Fat raindrops dance on the windshield, the man turns on the wipers. They creak and scrape in slow motion, then he flicks the switch again and they speed up to a hypnotic rhythm that matches the next song.

She knows this one: it's another of her daddy's favourites that she hasn't heard for years. They used to duet together whenever it came on the radio. Her daddy would sing the verse, and she would sing the doo-wop harmonies before joining in with him at the chorus. Before she can stop herself she finds she's singing those harmonies again, oh so softly. Hal lifts his head as if in warning and Mollie stops abruptly when she sees the man's face in the rear-view mirror.

Without changing expression he flicks on his turn signal and pulls in after the next intersection.

'Out,' he says quietly.

Mollie tries to catch his eye in the mirror, but he continues to stare straight ahead.

'I'm sorry – please give me one more chance. It won't happen again, I promise it won't. But that music is so good – it reminds me of home . . .' She tails off, finally catches his eye in the mirror.

'Mother?'

The woman nods. 'One more chance,' she says.

As they set off, she changes the radio station. Mollie assumes she's looking for something a little duller, something that won't provoke singing or chatter – perhaps a sports commentary or a news channel. The speakers fizz and crackle, blurting out brief phrases of music and conversation as the red needle moves slowly across to the right.

When she stops rotating the dial, the first notes of 'Dancing Queen' fill the car and the man reaches straight for the volume, turning it way up high. Mollie wells up, blinking furiously. This is the song she used to dance to with her mama, holding hands as they boogied around the kitchen. Now she stays silent as a delta of tears make tracks through the red dust on her cheeks. Hal looks up at her, sad-eyed, pawing gently at her leg, but neither of them make a single sound as the miles roll slowly by.

waited so long

The house is quiet without Mollie. Ella is aware of her footsteps echoing along the passageway, of the eerie creak of each and every floorboard, of the scuttle of dry leaves on the porch. She turns the radio way up loud to drown out the silence, to swallow up her worry and her guilt.

Sherman always makes it clear that the radio irritates him: the jingles and the advertisements, the repetitive news and traffic reports, the DJ talking over the end of the best songs.

But Ella never notices any of that. She loves the mellow tone of the big old radio that once belonged to Sherman's parents, the honeyed voices of her favourite DJs. They talk quietly to her in the evenings as though she's the only person listening. Now she is on her own she sits in the parlour and listens in the dark, the curtains drawn back so she can see Sherman's headlights when he comes around the last bend in the track. But since the day Mollie left, Sherman hasn't come home at all except to change his clothes.

When Ella was younger she always dreamed that one of her tenth grade boyfriends would call up the local radio station and request a song especially for her. Often she would drop hints when she sat with Petey Walls in the soda shop. She would hear a love song playing on the jukebox and twirl her hair around her finger as she gazed off into the distance, saying wouldn't it be just grand if someone you loved called up the *Quiet Moon Radio Show* to dedicate a request.

Back then, Ella slept with all the boys who asked her, so certain it was the way to their hearts. It worked at first, but then she'd come on too strong, let it be known she expected a wedding ring on her finger by the time she was eighteen, that she wanted a house by the shore on Sunset Street. And every time a boy ditched her she thought the next one would be different, that they'd fall in love with her just like in the movies.

Mr Clark had given her twenty dollars for taking her virginity in the back of his car – more money than she'd ever had before – and in return she'd promised to keep quiet. It hadn't been so bad anyhow. Mr Clark was a gentleman, had treated her kindly, kept telling her how pretty she was, how any man would be lucky to have her. There was no doubt some of her high school boyfriends would have done well to take note of his words.

After that night, Ella decided to grow her hair long so she could pin it up, started wearing eyeliner and lipstick and hanging out with the older girls. Something in her had changed for good, yet she always kept her promise and never told a soul about Mr Clark.

She bought a transistor radio with her twenty dollars, told her mother she'd saved up for it out of her birthday and Christmas money. She would go to bed with it hidden under the covers, turned way down low so her mama wouldn't hear, her ear pressed against the speaker. She imagined Petey Walls talking to the DJ, Bobby Deal, asking for a special song, telling him that it was for the girl who'd captured his heart. She pictured Bobby sitting in the studio all alone in a pool of golden light, a cup of coffee topped with hot milk on his desk, his headphones around his neck as he took the call.

When she was eighteen and met Phil Archer, they listened to the *Quiet Moon Radio Show* as they drove back from the movies or the diner, or when they parked up at the edge of the lake in the moonlight. After they'd made out in the back of Phil's father's car, he would watch her in silence as she reapplied her lipstick and fixed her hair, Bobby Deal's voice drifting out into the woods through the open window, carrying across the water as he played requests and read out the love stories of a dozen American teenagers just like them. And Ella would sigh, would say to Phil that it might well be the best thing ever if a boy you loved were to call up Bobby Deal and ask for that new song by Ray Terry. Phil would nod distractedly as he leaned out and combed his hair in the side mirror, and Ella would shiver inside, thinking of the title of that song: 'Waited So Long For A Girl Like You'. It said everything she wished Phil would say to her; just those few words were all she wanted to hear.

at the hairdresser's

Phil Archer and Janet Pearlman were given a second chance. Janet knew it was selfish and wrong to pursue it, but nevertheless she'd been sure from the start they would take it.

Not that she'd planned it, hadn't even known he was still around until she saw the sign above the boatyard door. She'd thought of him often over the years, wondered if he looked the same, if he was still thinking of her from time to time.

When she saw him cross the street to the barber's, her heart fluttered in its cage like a schoolgirl's. She picked up the sweeping brush and turned around so her back was to the door. He stood just inside, called out good morning to Ged and Ian.

'Morning, Phil! Be with you in ten minutes or so. Unless you'd like to try our new girl?'

He turned to the chair in the window, saw a woman sweeping up, a thick chestnut plait falling down her back. She turned and smiled.

'I saw you crossing the street,' she said. 'I'd have known you anywhere.'

She stood in sunlight, tanned and lean, feet firmly planted, as sure of her place in the world as she'd always been.

He walked straight over to her. 'Janet,' he said.

They stood in silence for a moment.

'You're back from Longfield?' he asked, said it as casually as though he'd been waiting only a week or so for her to return, as though she'd just been home to her parents' house for a few days.

'Not exactly – I still live down there, got a place of my own. But I'm working in here a few mornings a week now. Must be twelve or thirteen years since I last saw you? I hear you married Ella Jones, and you've got two kids now?'

He nodded and sat down in the chair. 'Mollie and Angel – Angel's the elder of the two. You got kids?'

She shook her head.

'Well maybe you did the right thing, they can be a real handful, that's for sure. Anyway, I'm at the boatyard most days. Do you still surf? Call in if you're around – we can catch up properly.'

'I might just do that if I'm ever down there. So, what is it to be today?'

'Just a trim please,' he said.

'Certainly.' She shook out a towel, placed it gently around his shoulders, and their eyes met in the mirror.

radio request

When Ella Archer's radio request finally came, it was after an argument. She felt as though she'd been married for a lifetime, and she was tired. Tired of working at the diner and trying to bring up two kids with very little help. Tired of her husband staying out after work with his friends, tired of hearing rumours about the new girl in the hairdresser's. She'd had plenty of offers herself over the last few years, but she'd always turned them down – well almost always. She'd come to love Phil more than she ever thought she would, and she'd tried her best. Yet she knew she'd pushed him too hard, trying to get him to expand the boatyard when he was happy with things as they were, always expecting more from him than he wanted to give. Sometimes it was clear as day that Phil Archer didn't want to be in that house on Sunset Street; she could see that the very heart of him was absent.

Ella knew her mother had been glad to see the back of her when she'd married Phil.

She'd been a wild teenager, skipping school, hanging out with an older crowd, drinking and smoking when she was barely fifteen. She'd always tried to act cool and smart, playing a part way older than her years, but when she argued with her parents she was still a petulant child. And they were often mystified by her strange behaviour; those things she did to spite or shock – like the time she cut off Olivia's hair and Mrs Clark had forced the Archers to pay some fancy hairdresser in Atlantic City to put it right.

They had no idea where they'd gone wrong. Although the Joneses weren't wealthy, Ella and her older sister had always had everything they wanted, and no one ever said a word to Ella when she came in late, her lipstick smeared and her blouse pulled loose. They didn't want to challenge her, to push her to rebel even further, so they thought it was best to remain quiet, hiding their constant fear she would fall pregnant.

As Ella moved through her teens, collecting promise rings as though they were candy, her mama could see that most of the other young girls were nothing like her daughter. They spent their time with their high school friends, went round to each other's houses to do their school work. When Ella piled on her make-up and backcombed her hair she looked five years older than the rest. When she was ready to go dancing she would seek out her mother wherever she was in the house, asking her if she thought she was beautiful. Her mother always said yes, yet Ella herself was aware that all she had was a cheap kind of prettiness, all surface and artifice.

So when Ella met Phil Archer, Mary and Arnie Jones were relieved – a nice boy from a good family, set to take on his uncle's boatyard. Yet Mary understood her daughter well enough to know it would never last. Ella had shown no interest in a career either; she trained in dressmaking after leaving school, had entertained notions of being a fashion designer or opening a boutique, yet nothing had come of it. There was a strange emptiness at the heart of her, coupled with a compulsion to vie for the attention of men, an urgent need to make them all fall in love with her. It was as though she felt worthless without that validation. Her mother could guess exactly how Ella had gone about claiming Phil Archer's affection, but she knew no one would ever love her daughter the way she craved.

Just two weeks ago, Ella had tried hard to make everything right. She'd persuaded Phil they should go out together on Sunday, take their son and daughter for a stroll along the boardwalk for the first time in months. But as they'd gone through the turnstile to the Tunnel of Love, Ella glimpsed the hairdresser from Ged's standing by the railing. She saw the girl wave at Phil, couldn't stop herself from saying something, and they'd argued in front of Mollie.

And earlier that evening she'd tried to make everything special, had cooked Phil his favourite meal, made sure Angel and Mollie were both at sleepovers. But they drank too much beer and argued again, going over and over the same old ground.

'Are you having an affair? Are you leaving me?' she asked. She almost whispered the words, as though by saying them quietly she could change the answer to 'no'.

'If you had any sense you would know,' he said.

Ella didn't reply, couldn't bear to hear him say it. She switched on the radio, turned the dial until she heard Bobby Deal's voice, then poured herself another beer. When she realised Phil wasn't going to continue the argument she decided to stay quiet, to give the evening another chance.

'I didn't know Bobby was still doing this show,' she said. 'It's so long since we've listened to the radio together. Do you remember when I liked that song they used to play all the time – the one by Ray Terry? I always wished you'd call up the station and get them to play it for me.'

Phil nodded, his face full of sadness and despair, watched his wife's face as she sang along to the radio. He sat quietly for a while, then nodded to himself decisively, stood up and left the room without a word. Ella drummed her fingers on the arm of the couch, thought of all the things she wanted to say to him. But the beer had diluted her reason, she could feel a hangover starting before she even went to bed.

She sat in silence as the next song played, didn't hear Phil come back into the room and stand behind her. When the music ended and she heard Bobby Deal say her name, Ella let out a tiny squeal of surprise. She jumped up, saw her husband standing in the corner gazing down at the floor, unable to look her in the eye.

'This one's for Ella Archer on the Jersey shore. Apparently she's always dreamed someone would request a song for her on my show. So Ella, this is your moment. Phil remembers when you were first together, how you always talked about a song by Ray Terry.'

She gasped and stood up, but as she walked towards Phil he tried to side-step her, lunging for the radio as though he'd changed his mind. She caught hold of his hand and stopped him, yet she was suddenly unsure.

'So here we go, Ella. This is from your husband. Better late than never.'

Phil pulled free of her and backed into the doorway. She was suddenly aware that the introduction to the song was all wrong. It was Ray Terry, but it wasn't 'Waited So Long For A Girl Like You'.

Phil saw her face fall, watched the twist of her features when she realised what was happening.

'They call this 'The Love That's Gone',' she said.

Phil shook his head, pressed his fingertips to his forehead, as though he could hardly believe what he'd done. He held his hands up. 'I'm really sorry, I shouldn't have done that. It was a stupid impulse. But things haven't been right for some time – we both know that. I've tried to tell you, I have . . .'

As he tailed off, Ella was sure she heard his voice break. He turned abruptly and left the room before she could see his face. Two days later he packed a large suitcase and walked out of the house for good.

a ride for your story

The road is straight as far as the eye can see, and in the distance Mollie makes out a blur of blue in a cloud of dust. She stands near the junction for the gas station, holding out her cardboard sign so drivers will see her as they turn in.

The blue car signals and slows down. She sees a woman at the wheel, wearing a silk head square and oversized shades as though she thinks she's Jackie Onassis. The car is a beauty: a Corvette with cream leather seats.

The driver's window opens smoothly with a faint, soft whir just as a pair of squabbling crows take flight. The woman smiles, looks Mollie up and down, takes in her dusty clothes, her sunburnt nose, the strands of loose hair escaping from her ponytail. The dog gets up from where he's been sitting in the shade under a scrawny bush, trots over to the car.

The woman shakes her head. 'No dogs,' she says.

Hal wags his tail, lifts his head up towards the open window and gives a gentle bark.

'Well I got an old blanket in the trunk, I guess he could sit on that if you'll vouch for him.'

'I'll vouch for him,' Mollie says.

'I'm heading for Anderton if you're going that way? Have you got any money for gas?'

Mollie shakes her head, takes a step backwards and stands on Hal's paw. He yelps and looks up at her. She rests her hand on the top of his head and turns back to the Corvette.

'No, sorry, I haven't. I have a few dollars, but I need that for food for Hal.'

'I'm only joking with you, kid – I don't need your money. I bet you got some interesting stories though? I'll trade you a ride for your story?'

Mollie smiles and reaches for the door handle.

'Don't forget the blanket in the trunk.'

The trunk clicks opens, and Mollie pulls out a red and green check rug that she lays across the back seat.

The woman drives fast, unnerving Mollie as she swerves sharply from lane to lane. She starts talking straight away, says her name is Alice Green, that she's driving back from some business she had to take care of in Texas.

'You running from a man?' she asks.

'I guess.'

'It's always the same story, kiddo. Say, what's your name anyhow?'

'Mollie. And he's Hal,' she adds, indicating the dog with a wave of her hand.

'Well, Millie–'

'Mollie.'

'Millie, Mollie, what's a name between friends?' She lets out a raucous laugh that causes Hal to yelp. 'Well, Mollie, tell me all about the bum.'

'He's my . . .' She pauses. It's too close, too raw, she's not sure she can share her story with a stranger yet.

Alice reaches across and puts her hand on Mollie's knee. She flinches involuntarily.

'Ah, now I got it, at least I think I do. Some older

guy – an uncle, or your father maybe?'

'Kind of a stepfather.'

Alice nods. 'You get away in time?'

'He beat me a little. But yeah, I guess.'

'And what about your mama? She know? She care?'

'She knows, and in her heart she cares. But Mama was too frightened to say a thing. She wanted to live in a big house, and now she doesn't want to lose face. I shouldn't have left her, but I just had to . . .'

'You got a real daddy anywhere? One of the good guys?'

'I do. I got a daddy and a brother too. His name's Angel. They're both my good guys.'

She turns round to check on Hal. He looks up at her and wags his tail.

'And I have Hal. He's my real good guy.'

'Do you want to know what I think, Millie-Mollie? I think you had a narrow escape, and I know you did the right thing in leaving. When you get home, you need to ask your daddy or your brother to help if you think your mother needs rescuing. I know you love her, but it really ain't your problem.

'Say, how 'bout you stay with me overnight? We can stop in Hanover at the Dream Inn, talk some more and head for Anderton in the morning. What d'you say? I'll get you a room of your own, we can have a nice meal someplace? Go dancing?'

'Well, I–'

'C'mon, it'll be fun. I need company and you need a bed and a lift. It's a fair trade. I can even do a detour, drop you off past Anderton before I head north

– I guess that'd be another fifty miles or so. And I'll slip you a few dollars to help you on your way. It's a win-win!'

'Okay . . . thanks.'

Alice reaches across, puts her hand on Mollie's arm. This time she doesn't flinch.

'I'll prove to you that us women can have far more fun without men!'

you get all that
from your mother

After Mollie's daddy moved to Longfield, he used to pick her up on alternate Sundays and take her out to lunch. There was only ever the two of them because Angel refused to see him.

They always went to Rosie's Diner and Mollie usually ordered the same thing – chicken served with fried green tomatoes, and an ice cream sundae to follow. Sometimes they rode on the old rollercoaster, the one which clattered and swayed alarmingly, scaring her more than the fancy new one that climbed up twice as high. But occasionally her daddy insisted on going on the Tunnel of Love instead. Mollie hated that ride now, but somehow she never got around to telling him.

It reminded her of the last time they went out before he left, that April Sunday when they were all together and Mama made them ride the Tunnel for old time's sake. Her brother said it was for sissies, so it was just the three of them, Mollie squashed up in the middle. When their boat rattled back out into the sunshine, Mollie could see Mama was crying and it seemed nothing Daddy said could make her stop. They walked away from her, exchanging fierce whispers, and two weeks later her daddy moved out.

When Mollie was younger she always blamed the ride for splitting them up, yet she could never quite figure out the why and the wherefore. And because she'd never dared mention it to Daddy, and he didn't seem to remember, she was forced to sit next to him, holding his warm hand as their love boat wound around the neon-lit caves of hearts and cherubs.

Occasionally they went down to Atlantic City to walk along the boardwalk there, and he'd buy her salt water taffy or cotton candy. He bought her a set of notecards and told her to write to him on the weekends he wasn't seeing her, yet Mollie could never think of anything to tell him. She wanted to say she missed him, that combing the beach wasn't the same on her own, that she had no one to help her with her chemistry homework, that Mama was hurting without him, that she didn't like Janet. But she never told him any of those things. The one time she'd said anything bad about Janet his face looked so sad she'd wanted to take it right back. But she didn't know how. It reminded her of Mama's sad face too, of her silent sobs as she paced back and forth across the porch.

'Mollie, sweetheart, I want you two to get on. Janet makes me happy.'

'Didn't Mama make you happy too?'

'She did once upon a time, but . . . well it's a little too complicated for you to understand. And you know I still love you and Angel just as much as I possibly could.'

'Well maybe Janet won't make you happy for long, and then you can come back to Mama again.'

'It doesn't really work that way, Mollie.'

'But Mama's sad. It's not right that you and Janet are happy when Mama isn't.'

'Your mother will be okay in time.'

'But Mama cries herself to sleep, and Angel is mad at you, and I hardly get to see you. It just isn't fair – I wish Janet had never come back here.'

He sighed and shook his head, unsure how to answer. Mollie's eyes glittered, and for a moment she looked just like her mother. He ruffled her hair and pulled her close to him, kissed the top of her head.

'You're a tough one, Mollie Archer, that's for sure. You're stubborn and you're outspoken, and you'll argue until you're blue in the face. But you're kind too, and funny. You have a good heart.'

He paused. 'You get all that from your mother.'

He fell silent then, and when Mollie looked up she saw him blink rapidly, just like she did herself when she was trying not to let anyone see her cry.

dancing queen

There's only one room vacant at the Dream Inn motel, but Mollie says she doesn't mind.

'It'll be more fun sharing anyway!' says Alice.

She pulls out a bottle of Jack and pours them each a large measure in the scratched plastic tooth mugs, lays her clothes on the bed and tells Mollie to pick out a T-shirt. She examines the array of glitter and sequins, selects a pale blue one embellished with angel wings. Alice sweeps the dust off her jeans with a clothes brush, lends her a pair of high-heeled boots and pronounces her ready to go.

Then she looks at Mollie's face and changes her mind. 'We need to make you look a little older if we can.'

She sits her down on the bed under the central light and fetches a palette of sparkly eyeshadows, mascara, a bright red lipstick. When she's finished, Mollie wants to look in the bathroom mirror, wants to borrow Alice's curling tongs to fix her hair, but she pushes her out of the door.

'No time, Millie-Mollie, we need to eat at the diner before it closes.'

Mollie admires her own reflection in the window as she eats her pork cutlet and fries; she looks different, older, and she wishes Chrissy could see her right now.

In the Red Rooster Roadhouse, Alice orders a pitcher of beer, pulls Mollie up to dance to almost every song. They dance to Steve Earle and Gloria Gaynor – Alice singing all the words to 'I Will Survive' at the top of her voice – to Tom Petty, Blondie, Lou Reed. The Jack Daniel's and the beer make Mollie brave; she catches Alice's enthusiasm, feels her face breaking into the widest smile. They dance together, just the two of them, ignoring the stares from the surrounding tables.

'I told you women have the most fun without men!' Alice shouts.

When they weave their way through the crowd to leave, Mollie blows a kiss at the man in the Stetson who was watching them dance, drapes her arm around a curly-haired boy who said hello when they first walked in.

'I'm just trying them out,' she says, as Alice drags her away.

They clatter across the car park, their heels still dancing, the sound amplified in the cool night air.

Back at the motel, Mollie collapses onto the bed, and Alice pulls off her boots, helps her take off her T-shirt and jeans. She turns down the covers and gets in behind her. Mollie can feel Alice's warm skin against her own, her soft breath on her neck.

'Goodnight, my dancing queen. We had fun didn't we?' she whispers.

Mollie pretends to be half-asleep, mumbles a reply, stays as still as she can, listening to her own heartbeat, wanting to feel Alice's skin against hers for as long as possible. She feels safe here, protected, as though someone is truly looking out for her.

Alice mutters something else she doesn't catch, her lips pressed against Mollie's shoulder, her arm curling around her waist. Mollie can feel Alice's breathing slow down as her own quickens. She is conscious of the weight of Alice's arm, the heat of her skin where their bodies touch, is aware of every nerve ending. Then Alice jerks awake, pulls her arm away as she rolls onto her back. Mollie lies in the dark, makes out the shapes of the wardrobe and the chair, feels a stir of emotions she doesn't understand: disappointment, relief, excitement, and that want again, the want of something she doesn't understand.

word perfect

It's late afternoon when Eddie stops for diesel and a coffee. There's a teenage girl in front of him in the line to pay. He caught a glimpse of her when he first walked through the door, filling a used bottle at the water fountain. She's buying a can of dog food and a sandwich, and he notices her re-checking the cash in her hand as she reaches the front of the line.

He can't help watching her as she counts out the coins so carefully. He hasn't seen her face except in profile, framed by a cloud of tangled hair tied up with a scrap of blue ribbon. Right now, she could be Zig. Same height, same build, same style khaki knapsack as Zig's schoolbag. He knows this girl won't be anything like his daughter when she turns around, but his heart still pounds as he waits for her to leave the counter. When she does turn, she looks straight at him, as though she's read his mind. She's a lot like Zig, more than he'd dared hope. Same wide mouth and dark eyes. But of course, it isn't her. And he's only disappointed for a few seconds, because he's used to it now. He last saw Zig a year ago, when she was barely fourteen, and though he tries to update her in his head, the memory that keeps returning is the one of that night when she was ten or eleven years old.

The three of them had set off back from the mall just as the snow became heavy. Zig was squashed up in the front seat of the pickup between him and Amber, Rollo the dog sitting on her knee. She begged him to stop in the woods so she could build a snowman, but it was already dusk and so her mother promised they could make one together the next morning instead. Eddie turned up the radio when he heard 'Thunder Road', glanced across at Amber over the top of Zig's head. Impulsively, he stopped at the side of a clearing, cranked the volume even higher and jumped out of the cab, soft, fat flakes settling on his hair and shoulders. He opened the passenger door, held out his hand to his wife.

'Will you dance with me?' he asked, grinning.

They tumbled out into the swirl of white and danced together in the headlights, Rollo prancing around them in circles, his paws making patterns in the snow. Zig pushed between them and held both of their hands in her mittened ones, twirling, laughing, as the flakes fell thicker and faster.

Then Amber stumbled, gasping and clutching her stomach. Eddie carried her to the car, drove quickly to the hospital, cradled Zig's snow-wet head in his hands and reassured her over and over that her mother would be fine. And after the blood and the tears, the loss of the child they had never known, there came the recriminations, the silence, and then the shouting.

Nothing was ever the same, and Zig came to believe that a dead baby, no bigger than a walnut, had somehow become more important to her parents than their living child. Their lost baby was the elephant, the ghost, in every room. And so she left home, disappeared when she was just fourteen, and now Eddie's heart breaks for her every day.

The girl with the dog hesitates a moment before heading to the exit road with her cardboard sign. She stops, takes out her sandwich, empties the can of dog food into the empty carton and watches as he wolfs it down. Trucks rumble by as they leave the parking lot, each one blocking out the low afternoon sun as they pass. She looks up as she hears the hiss of brakes, sees Eddie's elbow resting on the open cab window, his wrist wrapped twice round with a plaited leather bracelet.

'You wanting a ride?' Eddie smiles at her, leans further out of the window, and the white face of a Jack Russell appears at his side.

'I can appreciate you might be worried accepting a ride from me – a guy on his own – but this here is Rollo, and he won't stand for no funny business. Who's that you got with you?'

'Hal,' she says. 'I've got Hal to protect me. And I'm Mollie.'

'Pleased to meet you, Hal and Mollie. I'm Eddie. Where exactly are you heading?'

'East,' she says. 'As far east as you can get.'

'I'm going the slow route, heading to Craven, then Jonesborough. That do you, or anywhere on the way?'

Mollie tries to remember the route she planned out on Sherman Rook's map. 'Anywhere's good as long as it helps me get to New Jersey.'

'Oh I can take you across the state line and more – fifty miles from the shore, maybe. And if you want to tell me why you're running to the coast then I'm all ears, but if you don't then I can bore you with my life story instead.'

Mollie is still doubtful. But she wants this ride so badly; it's the ride that will get her very nearly home. Eddie sees her doubt, wishes he could prove his intentions. He wants to help her, wants to protect her, just as he wants someone to look out for Zig.

'What do you think, Hal?'

The dog wags his tail, and Mollie takes it as a good sign.

'Hal says yes!'

They climb up into the cab, and Hal settles down in the back with Rollo. Eddie pulls down the sun visor and two photos tumble out. One is of a pretty woman a little older than Mollie's mama. The other is of a girl, maybe thirteen or fourteen, eyes narrowed against the sun, a gap between her front teeth.

'My daughter, Zig, and her mother.'

He hands them over to her and Mollie can see the photos make him sad.

'Your best girls?' she asks quietly.

'My best girls,' he says, but he doesn't meet her eye. Then he reaches for a box of cassettes behind him and passes it across to her. 'Do you like music? Pick something out.'

When Eddie hears the first notes of 'Thunder Road', a sadness pulls his face tight, then he looks at Mollie's smile and makes a decision, puts the truck into gear and turns the volume way up high. They sing along together, word perfect, and Hal lets out a single yowl like a wild coyote.

mercury in retrograde

As Mollie passes Madame Zara's fortune-telling booth, the old woman sticks her head out of the door, her cheap hoop earrings catching the late afternoon sunlight.

'Mollie Archer, is that you?'

Mollie pauses, remembers the time Zara told her mama she'd meet the love of her life at the Ocean Club dance. Mama bought a new dress and spent $20 on a ticket she could ill afford. Zara promised her a wealthy man as tall, dark and handsome as cliché would allow, said she could see him at the Little Magnolia wedding chapel with her mama stood right at his side.

The dance had been a humiliating failure, the doorman mistaking her for a hooker when she sat at the bar counter too long, and Mollie and Angel had to eat plain crackers and catering hot dogs for the next two weeks while Mama made the money back.

'So you're home safe? We all thought you were happy out west with yer mama and that fancy new man of hers? What you got a dog for now anyhow? You seen your brother yet?'

Mollie smiles at the rapid questions. 'You'll have to read my fortune if you want to know what happened – tell me that Mercury is in retrograde and that a man with green eyes will be the bearer of good news?'

She sees Zara's dark eyes light up at the promise of gossip, the hard glitter of them in the half-light of the booth's interior. She sniffs, takes hold of Mollie's arm, then waves her inside.

Mollie perches on the low velvet couch where

she used to sit as a child, quietly listening to Zara as she read her mama's cards, fascinated by the way her cheap lipstick bled into the lines around her mouth.

'Your brother has moved in with that Italian girl from Pacitto's ice cream parlour, and your daddy is still down at Longfield.'

'Well I could have told you that, Zara. Angel and Daddy have been writing to me the whole time I've been away.'

'Not this last few days they haven't, because nobody knows where you've been. Your daddy's been up here asking questions, and your mama has phoned everyone she knows in this town. She know where you are now?'

Mollie doesn't answer. She moves over to the table and holds out her hand. Zara leans forward, grasps it between both of her own, her bangles clattering heavily against the metal top. She runs her thumb back and forth across the girl's palm, then sighs dramatically.

'You've been on a long journey to get back here.'

Mollie raises an eyebrow.

'People have been kind and people have been mean . . . and sometimes you seen things you shouldn't.'

She looks up at Mollie and waits, as though she expects encouragement to continue. Mollie stays silent, turns around as she hears the piercing shrieks of two young boys. They race past the window clutching kites: a red eagle, a neon green fish, both with long tails that whip around their faces in the warm wind.

'You stole a truck.'

'Yeah, well I guess my mama will have told everyone that.'

'And then there's the dog. That dog has saved your life.'

'How do you mean?'

'Well if it wasn't for you caring about the dog you wouldn't have gotten away from the farm. And he's been there for you all the way hasn't he?' She squeezes Mollie's hand. 'I can see him now in a dusty yard somewhere, an old car with the door open, a man pushing you inside.'

Mollie snatches her hand back and jumps up, but Zara keeps talking.

'And that dog has his teeth clamped around the man's ankle. I can hear shouting, see someone running out of the house, but they don't find you.'

Mollie gasps. 'How can you know all that? No one knows what happened there except me. I haven't told a soul.'

'Well you said I had to read your fortune to find out what happened, and so that's what I've done. I could see it all.'

Mollie jumps up and paces around the booth, can feel her heart racing.

'Well you may know what happened to me on my journey home – though I don't know where you got it from – but my fortune is the future, not the past. So what happens next? That's the hard part.'

Zara laughs her brittle laugh, takes a cigarette from a pack on the window ledge and flicks open her lighter. She takes a long drag, exhales slowly.

'I'll tell you just one thing, Mollie. You can't move on until you let go of your needless guilt about your friend. You couldn't have saved her, it wasn't your fault she went driving with Sam Madden. It was Chrissy's choice. You need to face up to it, let your grief out, not bury all those feelings away.'

She reaches for Mollie's hand, waits for her to sit down again.

'And d'ya know, to be truthful, I've never understood folks wanting to find out their futures. Why colour everything you do with the burden of knowing what happens next? We all know nobody gets out alive.'

Mollie nods. 'Yeah, I always thought fortune-telling was overrated. Good or bad, I want to greet every day as a surprise.'

'You always were a sensible kid, Mollie Archer. But if you need to know anything, then I'm always here.'

'Okay, square with me now. How did you know all that stuff about me? Do you really think you have a psychic gift?'

Zara shrugs. 'Sometimes I see things – just random jumbled scenes in my head, like a dream I guess. And sometimes those things have happened, or they do happen afterwards, but other times they're just my crazy thoughts. Only last night I was watching the TV, some old Ronald Reagan movie, and I suddenly saw him as our next president. Sat there in the White House he was – I saw it clear as day.'

'Well you better keep that one to yourself – or at least don't tell my daddy that!'

Zara holds something out in her hand. 'Cross my palm with silver for a lucky charm to protect you.'

Mollie pulls two quarters from her pocket and places them on the table, takes the fake fur rabbit paw and looks out through the window at the pale sand and the rushing clouds. It feels like a year since she's been away, yet it's less than two months. She can sense an imperceptible shift, is aware of everything being different now. Yet she knows it's her who's changed; the Jersey shore is just the same as it ever was.

When she leaves Zara's booth she takes the steps down to the beach, kicks off her boots and carries them down to the shoreline. She gasps as the cold shallows lap around her ankles, watches the boys' kites pull and tug on their lines. She throws a piece of driftwood for Hal, and when he drops it at her feet she picks it up again. Yet before she throws it a second time she crouches down and writes 'Chrissy' in the firm sand at the water's edge. Mollie watches the waves roll in over the letters and rush back out again, whispers her friend's name as she watches it blur and fade.

the bus to the shore

Saul Bradshaw has never taken a trip away without one of his parents.

Sure, he's been for days out with Nile and Harry – lake fishing, swimming, or a drive up to Nile's cousin's house for something to do. But he's never taken a proper trip where he's stayed away overnight.

He sits at Sherman Rook's desk and places the mud snail shell on the jotter, imagines the crash of waves and sand as fine as icing sugar. He opens out one of the old linen roadmaps, looks up the route that leads to New Jersey. He's saved some money since starting work at the car lot and he's been thinking about renting a place of his own, or buying a better car. But there's something about that late August afternoon, the golden light at the turn of the season, that makes him want to get away for a while. Saul remembers the cries of the seagulls, thinks of Mollie Archer's soft skin and dark eyes, and knows he wants to spend his money on a trip to the shore. He thinks about telling his mama, about ringing his Aunty Jenny, but then he decides this is something he wants to do all on his own. His mama will only criticise his plans, say she can't manage without him, and if he stops with Aunty Jenny then it won't be the same as staying in a hotel and doing exactly as he wants to do.

He considers taking his car, imagines picking Mollie up at the roadside, driving across the country on empty roads, the windows wound down, Mollie's hair tied up with a bright red scarf, the radio blasting out their favourite songs. Yet in truth he knows his old Ford wouldn't make it all that way.

The next morning he heads over to the local bus station, finds out the best route to take, buys a round-trip ticket to New York City leaving early Monday morning. From there he'll take the local bus from Port Authority down to Atlantic City. He could take the bus to Philadelphia and then a train or bus to the shore, but this way he gets to see the bright lights of New York, even if it's only for a few hours.

And then he'll head down the New Jersey Turnpike and find Mollie Archer.

Ella Archer has nothing with her save for hope and a tote bag full of clothes. While she waits at the roadside in Oakridge for the St Louis bus, she keeps her head low, turns up her shirt collar, hopes that no one acquainted with Sherman will drive by.

In St Louis she climbs aboard a Greyhound bus that will take her all the way through to New York. When the woman at the ticket counter asks if she's planning on going to Philadelphia or NYC, she pauses for a moment. She knows they'll end up costing pretty much the same, knows that it would be quicker to travel via Philly, but her sister lives in New York City and now seems as good a time as any to pay her a visit.

She'd made her decision to leave the night before, and early that morning she looked around Mollie's room for the last time. The door was splintered where the bolt still hung loose and pieces of dog kibble crunched beneath Ella's feet. She straightened the rug, lay down on Mollie's bed and rested her head on the pillow, breathed in the warm grass scent of her, pictured the dust and sunlight in her tangled hair. She realised she hardly knew her daughter any more, yet being in this room brought her suddenly close again. Ella felt fiercely proud of her, proud she'd had the courage to leave Oakridge and – as she'd just found out from one of their old neighbours – proud she'd made it safely home.

There was a glass on the chest of drawers, filled with dirty paint water and a splayed brush. She picked up the watercolour box, the squares muddied and almost used up, wondered what she'd been painting, what she thought of Ella, what she wanted for herself. She hoped upon hope that Mollie wouldn't end up like her, throwing a decent life away for some stupid dream.

She stood up then and went into her own room, packed a few things inside an old leather tote, took out the small roll of notes she'd hidden at the bottom of the laundry basket.

Ella knows she's let Mollie down, but she's determined to make it up to her now. She'll start that dressmaking business she always dreamt of as a child, open a boutique on the boardwalk, or maybe go back to college and learn to touch type and take down shorthand. It isn't too late to be someone, to set an example to Mollie.

What had she been chasing anyway? She'd been seduced by a hopeless dream of a new life; a life in a big house with a man who'd turned out to be bad to the bone. She couldn't change him or save him, any more than he could save her. The only thing Ella needed saving from was herself, and at least Sherman Rook had finally taught her what she didn't want, what she could do without.

She'd always craved attention and adoration, allowed real love to slip away unnoticed while she searched in vain for something more than she already had. When she finally got around to appreciating Phil, it was already too late.

Yet she knows it's the future that's important now, not the past, and she's certain she can do anything she wants if she puts her mind to it.

Things are going to be different.

Ella stands on the porch with her bag on her shoulder, takes a deep breath, sees that it's another beautiful day. She steps forward, then hesitates on the top step and looks back at the house. She shakes her head as though she knows she's being a fool, then turns around and unlocks the door, goes back inside. She picks up the phone in the hallway and calls Benny Dee, asks if he's found anyone permanent to run the Jupiter yet. Benny says he's been waiting for her call, and they both laugh.

She promises herself it will just be a stopgap this time, a few months at most.

Things are going to be different.

his father's fists

Early on Tuesday morning Sherman Rook walks across the yard to his front door. He hasn't been home since Saturday, unwilling to face Ella's silent tears and handwringing, especially right now, when the new barmaid at Lily Brown's is keeping a bed warm for him. Who'd have thought she would have turned out to be such good company? She could be the one to save him.

He smiles to himself at the thought of her. He'll take a bath, get Ella to iron his favourite shirt and then he'll go back down there.

It still upsets him to think Mollie got one over on him, but he got his truck back in one piece, and at least the girl has gone now. She was more trouble than she was worth in the end, so her departure was a silver lining.

Doesn't hurt to remind Ella Archer of her daughter's sins though, to keep her in her place. He unfastens his belt as he climbs the steps to the porch, whips it out through the loops and drags the buckle end along the hallway as he walks through to the kitchen.

The room is empty, the worktops cleared, the table scrubbed clean.

'Ella!' he calls. 'Where are you hiding?'

The house is silent, tidy, nothing out of place, and he walks from room to room, the scrape of the buckle echoing through the quiet space. He goes into their bedroom last of all, opens the door slowly, coils the belt around his hand, sure he'll find her there. He imagines her crouched in the corner, waiting for him.

He can see her face, the expression of faint defiance that maddens him so much, that makes him want to go on hitting her over and over again. She never cries, never holds her hands up to protect herself, never flinches.

The wardrobe is open, revealing a row of empty hangers, and in the mirror inside the door he catches sight of his father, a face filled with anger and hate, shoulders hunched, right fist thrust forward, wrapped twice round with the heavy, studded strip of leather. He recoils and drops the belt, holds his hands up to shield his head from his pa's fists, then falls down onto his knees and buries his face in the eiderdown so he can no longer see his cold eyes.

He can hear a low keening, primeval and unstoppable, doesn't register the sound as being of his own making until he feels the wet quilt beneath his cheeks. When a coyote howls in reply from somewhere across the valley, Sherman Rook looks up, understands for the first time that no one can save him except himself.

mollie & hal

Down on the north beach a girl and a dog race along the shoreline; the dog a streak of red against the pale sand and the white spume. He chases his tail, circles the girl, jumps awkwardly over the waves as though they're something solid. If anyone was to take a bet on it they'd probably wager that the dog had never seen the sea before. His paw prints crisscross the damp sand at the water's edge in skittering arcs, and the girl picks up a piece of driftwood and scratches out two names inside a heart.

Mollie and Hal.

The dog pauses to watch her, lunges for the stick, thinking it's some kind of game. The girl laughs at him and the dog grins back.

A hundred yards away, leaning on the boardwalk railings, a young man watches them, blonde hair blowing over his eyes in the strong breeze. He's near-sighted, too vain to wear his glasses unless he has to, and for a moment he thinks the girl could be his sister. Since his mama phoned to let him know she'd gone missing, he's seen her every day. In the grocery store there's always a girl with her messy corn-pale hair or her dark eyes; in the diner there'll be a girl with the same long matchstick legs or wide smile; in the office at the scrap yard there's a girl balanced precariously between childhood and womanhood who blushes when a boy glances her way for too long. Yet none of them have the thing, the extra thing that makes his sister so special – that soft light which radiates from her, that makes people turn and look twice even though they're not quite sure why.

This girl looks just like Mollie from a distance: yet he knows it can't be her. His sister doesn't have a dog, and the last he knew she was a thousand miles from the Jersey shore.

He punches the wooden railing, suddenly ashamed that he hasn't driven out west to look for her. When his mama phoned she sounded scared, yet he kept on dismissing her panic, told her he was sure Mollie would turn up back at Oakridge within a couple of days.

The girl is racing towards him along the beach now, oblivious to his presence, veering off to the left to climb the steps up to the boardwalk. She takes them two at a time, the dog's nails slipping on the slick treads, wood polished smooth by thousands of feet and a century of wind-blown sand.

'Let's get salt water taffy,' she says, pausing to scratch the dog behind his ear. 'And one of those tall banana shakes from Rosie's Diner.'

The man hears her voice, is reminded of all those Sundays his sister met their daddy for brunch at Rosie's while he stayed at home, sulking, unable to forgive his father for leaving them. All that time wasted.

The girl notices him for the first time as she draws level, almost trips over an empty soda bottle as she comes to an abrupt halt.

He grins at her, yet at first neither of them speak.

'Who's this then?' he asks as he reaches down to stroke the dog.

'His name is Hal,' she says. Hal jumps up, catching her off balance, sending the three of them crashing into the railings.

Mollie laughs as she throws her arms around her brother's neck, and he can feel her tears against his cheek.

acknowledgements

Once again I'm incredibly grateful to Consuelo Rivera-Fuentes and the brilliant team at Victorina Press for making this book happen, to Triona Walsh for another fabulous cover design, and to Mr L for all his love and support. Huge thanks to all the writers, reviewers and bloggers who are so generous with their time and words.

Crossing the Lines began life as 'Red', the story which was a runner-up in the 2018 Costa Short Story Award and subsequently published in my collection, *Scratched Enamel Heart*. I'd like to say thank you to all the readers who wanted to know what happened next and encouraged me to find out.

about the author

Amanda Huggins is the author of the novella, *All Our Squandered Beauty*, which won the 2021 Saboteur Award for Best Novella, as well as four collections of short fiction and poetry. Her travel writing, fiction and poetry have been widely published in anthologies, travel guides, newspapers and magazines. Her short stories have also been broadcast on BBC radio.

She has won several awards for her travel writing, most notably the BGTW New Travel Writer of the Year in 2014, and has been listed and placed in numerous short story and poetry competitions, including Bridport, Bath, and the Alpine Fellowship Award. In 2018 she was a runner-up in the Costa Short Story Award, and in 2020 she won the Colm Toibin International Short Story Award, was included in the BIFFY50 list of Best British and Irish Flash Fictions, nominated for a Pushcart Prize, and her poetry chapbook, *The Collective Nouns for Birds*, won the Saboteur Award for Best Poetry Pamphlet. In 2021 she won the H E Bates Short Story Competition and was a runner-up in the Fish Short Story Prize.

Amanda grew up on the North Yorkshire coast, moved to London in the 1990s, and now lives in West Yorkshire. She is a creative writing tutor and freelance editor.